# CHAPTER ONE

WHEN I WAS LITTLE, I thought that people died when they used up all their words. I thought everyone was born with a certain number of words and when they used them up, it was time for them to die. Not everyone was born with the same number. That would be too easy. You never knew how many words you were born with. That's why some people talked more than others and didn't die young. They had just been born with more words.

"Let my mom have been born with lots," I prayed. "Lots more than she's used."

I walked into my mother's hospital room. She was sitting up, talking to the woman lying in the next bed.

"Hi, sweetie. I'm so glad to see you," Mom said, opening her arms wide for my hug. "This is my daughter, Mindy. This is Ethel."

I smiled at Ethel, who had a patch over her left eye. She smiled and waved.

"She has no family," my mother whispered to me. "She's been here for a week with no visitors. I'm trying to keep her spirits up." She turned and gave Ethel a big smile. "Can my Mindy get you anything?"

"No, thanks." She spoke very slowly, as if we were foreigners. "She looks just like you," Ethel said, and rolled herself over, so that her back faced us.

"How has school been, sweetie?" my mother asked.

"Same," I said.

"And how is Gail?"

"Same." I should be nicer, I thought. I should be more chatty. "I've been sending away for college applications," I said.

"That's nice, sweetie."

She wasn't really listening. Her big brown eyes looked watery. She was staring at me, as if seeing me for the first time or as if she were seeing something else.

"Funny," she said. "I never thought you looked like me. I always thought you were so beautiful." She smiled. "Madame Lebrun and her daughter."

Years ago I would sit on my mother's lap as she sat at her vanity, putting on her makeup. I would sit very still, staring into the mirror, watching her as she finished applying lipstick. Then she would put her arms around me, her cheek right next to mine, and we would look at each other in the mirror.

"Madame Lebrun and her daughter," we would say together, and smile at our reflections. My mother told me it was a very famous painting, Madame Lebrun and her daughter. I had never seen it.

She turned to her bedside table and picked up her hairbrush. "Could you brush my hair for me, sweetie? I can't seem to do it, and it's all sticking up on the side."

"Sure," I said. I took the brush and started to touch it to her hair. I stopped. What if I jiggle the tumor? What if I bump her head and make the tumor worse? Should her head be touched at all? Should I ask the doctor if it's okay to brush her hair? My mother turned her head to me.

"Are you okay?" she said.

"Fine, Mom. Fine."

I started to brush, very lightly, trying to brush the hair without rubbing any of her scalp.

"That feels great, sweetie," she said. I could see her shoulders relax as I brushed.

Her hair was stiff, greasy, as if it hadn't been washed in a while. I couldn't brush down the sticking-out parts. They popped right back up every time. My fingers and wrist grew stiff from the effort.

"That was wonderful, sweetie. Thanks," she said.

I put the brush on her table.

"When they let me out of here, we'll go clothes shopping," she said. "This year we'll go to New York and eat lunch at Lord & Taylor's, in the Bird Cage. We'll eat *traife*—maybe shrimp—and we won't tell your father. And then we'll have ice cream for dessert." She giggled and snuggled down into her bed, turning on her side.

"I'm a little tired now, sweetie. I think I'll rest." She closed her eyes, then opened them. "I love you very much," she said, and went to sleep.

I sat watching her for a while. The cowlicks were still there. Did she know how many times she had called me sweetie? Were they going to shave her whole head?

Was the tumor making her do that, repeat the word *sweetie*? If it got worse, would that be the only word she could say? Would she remember all her sayings? "Everyone has his faults" was one. The whole phrase was "Everyone has his faults, and mine is being wicked." It was a quote from *The 13 Clocks* by James Thurber. She bought the book for me when I was five and read it to me over and over. "That's what makes horse races" was another. It always made me wonder what did make horse races. The horses? The jockeys?

The people who owned the horses? The people who bet on the horses? "At home we have it with whipped cream and nuts" was her favorite. My mother's aunt Bessie used to say it mournfully every time she was served Jell-O.

Did Mom know that she had a brain tumor? I had never asked, and my father had never said. I had no idea what she thought was wrong with her. What had they told her? I was glad she was asleep. I was afraid I might blurt out "BRAIN TUMOR" if I opened my mouth.

∾

My father walked in. "We'll let her sleep," he announced. He glanced at my mother and walked out of the room. I followed. I knew he had been talking with her doctor, but he said nothing, and I knew better than to ask. He hated it when I asked questions. He would tell me when he wanted to, because he wanted to. What I wanted didn't matter.

We drove the hour home to Roseville in silence, my father and I. I closed my eyes and pretended to sleep. It was easier than sitting there, not saying anything, when there was so much to be said.

We used to play games on our car trips, Geography, Twenty Questions. I'd sit in the front seat, by the window. My mother sat in the middle and fed me potato chips. She said the salt would keep me from getting carsick. It did.

One trip we stopped to ask the man in the car next to us for directions. "Follow me," he yelled through the open window.

We pulled into the lane behind him and followed him until we saw the sign we had been looking for and turned off. We all waved frantically, but he never noticed. The next morning, as we got into the car for the last leg of our trip, I asked, "Do you think that man still thinks we're following him?"

We all laughed and laughed. "Do you think that man still thinks we're following him?" we would ask one another.

Now there was a tumor in my mother's brain, inside her head.

I had always pictured my mother's head filled with file folders, all organized alphabetically, each holding precisely the papers it should hold, each file in its correct place. A place for everything and everything in its place.

Now some ugly, slimy bug had started to gnaw at the file folders, had pulled them apart, tossing thoughts and memories around until they made no sense, no connections. This thing had disrupted her filing system and was eating its way through the papers of her mind. I imagined the doctors opening up her skull and trying to get their hands on this demon who had grown fat, gorging on my mother's well-ordered mind.

∾

Close to home, my father and I drove to the drive-in that had just opened on Seneca Street. McDonald's. It would be fast; we could just pick up the food and eat it on our way.

I ordered a hamburger and french fries. My father kept kosher. There was nothing there he could eat.

"I'll stop at the delicatessen," he told me. "Nookie will make me a hot pastrami on rye."

The hamburger was skinny and smaller than the bun, the ketchup and pickles already on it. The french fries were long, thin, and limp. Everything came wrapped up in greasy paper. My father pulled out his gold money clip and peeled off a hundred-dollar bill. He always did that. He never carried ones or fives or tens. It was always hundreds. The cashier had to ask two other cashiers for help making change. We got back in the car. There wasn't enough ketchup, and the pickles were sweet. At home we have it with whipped cream and nuts, I thought.

This was not what dinners were supposed to be like.

Dinners happened at the dinner table, in our dining room. And they always began the same way.

"What's the scuttlebutt at the Imperial?" my mother would ask, flapping out her sparkling white, ironed napkin and placing it in her lap.

My father never said a word until my mother asked him that question. That was his introduction. Mom was the MC, turning the floor over to him, the Keynote Speaker. As if we had all agreed that we wanted to hear him speak. My father, the Speaker of our House. The only Speaker.

"Harry says business has been terrible the last week or so. No one buys furniture in the summer. I had Dover sole. Ben had lasagna. Murray had shrimp scampi. He raved about it."

My father would go on, describing every detail of his lunch and then every detail of his day.

"On my way back to the office, I was just in time to feed the meter. Two minutes to spare. Good timing."

My mother listened to every word. She nodded and even asked questions.

"Was it raining when you came back from lunch?"

I would sit silently, cutting my food into tiny pieces. He never asked about her day or about mine.

"That food reminds me of the crap they used to

8

feed us in the army," my father was saying about my hamburger and fries.

I had heard this story a million times.

"Part of the reason I organized an integrated cafeteria. The food was terrible. Of course, it didn't start out being integrated, Neenie."

Neenie. When I was little, I had called myself Neenie, and it stuck. My mother, my father, and all my relatives called me Neenie. But when I started nursery school and my teacher, Mrs. Butler, called me Mindy, I told my mother that's what I wanted to be called from then on.

"My real name. I want to be called by my real name."

"Fine," she had said. "Mindy it is."

"Can you ask Daddy to call me Mindy, too? He never does. He says he forgets."

"I'll ask," she had said, "but he loves Neenie. He may not be able to change."

He never did. "You will always be Neenie to me."

He was looking at me. I wasn't being a good audience. "Neenie?"

"Yes?"

"Everything was segregated in Georgia back then. And everyone I hired to work for me had no place to eat. So I set up a cafeteria just for them. But I made sure that the food was better than in the white cafeteria and bingo, in just a few short months, integration!"

How did my mother listen to these stories over and over? Didn't she ever want to tell her own? Take the floor herself?

"Sometimes they called me the Abraham Lincoln of the base, Neenie." He laughed as he pulled into the parking lot behind the delicatessen.

Neenie. Always Neenie.

# Chapter Two

THE NEXT MORNING I drove my mother's car to the library. I loved the library. I felt safe there. My mother used to bring me to Reading Hour every Sunday until I was eight. I pulled the heavy glass door open and walked in. That wonderful smell. I breathed deep. And then I heard Mrs. Redmond reading to the little kids who sat on the red Persian rug in the reading room, enthralled, as I had always been, by Mrs. Redmond's voice. "Hundreds of cats, thousands of cats," I heard them all whisper in unison, their eyes staring at Mrs. Redmond's soft, intelligent face.

"Millions and billions and trillions of cats," someone whispered in my ear.

I jumped. It was Bobby, the new kid in my class, the one from New York City.

"Sorry, I didn't mean to scare you," he whispered.

"How could I be scared listening to Mrs. Redmond?

The atom bomb would be deflected by her voice. This is the safest place in the world."

"You came here as a kid?" he asked.

"Every Sunday. I made my mother drive me here, no matter what. Sometimes she didn't even get dressed. She put on her coat over her nightgown. 'Pray we don't get into an accident,' she would say. 'I can't go to the hospital like this.' I never understood it. The hospital would just put her in one of their nightgowns. What did they care?" We laughed.

We were laughing about my mother. But it was good, it was okay.

"Did she read you *Ferdinand*?" Bobby asked.

"Yes," I said.

"That was my favorite," he said. " 'And for all I know he is sitting there still, under his favorite cork tree, smelling the flowers just quietly.' "

"And Horton?" I asked.

" 'I meant what I said, And I said what I meant,' " Bobby whispered.

" 'An elephant's faithful one hundred percent,' " I whispered back. We both whisper-laughed.

I barely knew Bobby. And here I was talking to him like he was my oldest friend.

"What are *you* doing here?" I asked him. God, I sounded like the Inquisition.

"Trying to start on my senior thesis."

Bobby didn't seem to mind.

"I won't have much time in the winter. I'm going out for basketball. So I need to get a head start on the paper." He smiled. "And you?"

"Me? No, I don't play basketball. Punchball at camp sometimes. Volleyball."

"No. I meant, why are you here?"

"Oh. Same thing. Senior thesis." Liar. You don't even have a topic.

"Well, see ya," he said, and headed toward the main reading room.

I listened to Mrs. Redmond a little longer, and then I settled in at a table by the window in the children's room. I looked at the shelves. I had read every book in this room, or my mother had read them to me.

She loved Dr. Seuss. She would speed up the pace and read, ever so distinctly, all the contortions of *If I Ran the Zoo, If I Ran the Circus, Scrambled Eggs Super!* But my favorite had been *Bartholomew and the Oobleck.*

I sat on the floor and found the Dr. Seuss section. There was old King Derwin, stuck in the oobleck, hoisted on his own petard, whatever that meant. I read it through, hearing my mother's voice, especially the chants of the wise men. She loved that part. And then there was Horton, sweet, old, faithful Horton the elephant. I picked up the book and got mad all over again when that Mayzie bird flew in to claim her baby, her baby that she had spent no time caring for or even thinking about. And then that picture, that incredible picture, where the egg bursts open and the truth is revealed: the truth of the nurturing, the truth that it is Horton's baby, because he cared for it. I looked at that picture, with the elephant-bird perched on Horton's trunk and everyone cheering, and I burst into tears, right there on the floor of the children's room of the library. And I couldn't stop. I grabbed my coat and pocketbook and ran out the back door to the car, sat there in the driver's seat, and sobbed and sobbed.

Last August, we had been walking down this street, heading for the Town Shoppe to buy a dress for Rosh Hashanah.

"I think a pink dress would be perfect," my mother said. "Something like that pretty dress you had for your Bas Mitzvah."

"I hated that dress," I said. The sleeves had pinched my arms in the middle so they looked like links of sausage.

"Why? You looked lovely in that dress."

And the waistband scratched.

"I hated that dress," I repeated through clenched teeth.

"But you loved the way the skirt twirled, don't you remember?" She stopped in the middle of the street to get a better look at me. I stopped, too.

"No, I hated it. But it doesn't matter. Let's go." I just wanted to get this shopping expedition over with.

"It does matter." Her voice was rising. "It matters to *me!*" She stomped her foot. "It matters to me!" She was screaming.

Now I had done it—again. She was going to have one of her fits. They were always my fault and I never knew when they were coming and we never talked about them afterward. They just happened, and then they were gone. I always caused them. I looked at my feet. People walked by us. At least their feet did. I watched a lot of feet go by.

"It matters! No one listens to me. This is no way to live. I can't stand it anymore." She was still screaming and now also crying. I pretended I didn't know her, that she was some crazy lady who had accosted me. And she was. What had I said that was so terrible? That I hadn't liked my Bas Mitzvah dress?

"I can't live like this. It matters to me. It matters, and no one listens." Her fists were balled up, and her right foot was stamping. I kept my head down. I had learned that if I looked at her directly during one of these fits, I would laugh. I don't know why. It wasn't funny. But I couldn't help it. Every time this happened I would laugh. And that would send her further away, further inside her own head. She yelled out at me from there.

"I never talked to *my* mother the way you talk to me. Never! She would have killed me. What did I do to deserve this? A daughter like my own mother? What did I do? When do I get to be the boss?" She was getting to the end. As soon as she started screaming about her mother and how much I was like her, that meant it would end soon.

I kept my eyes down. If I looked at her and laughed now, it would start her up all over. I bit my lower lip. Don't laugh, I repeated to myself. Just don't laugh.

I drove home from the library and called Gail.

"Can you come over?" I begged.

"You okay?"

"Yes. No, not really. I just read *Horton Hatches the Egg* and sobbed so hard I had to leave the library."

"Library?" she asked.

"Children's room," I said.

"The part where the elephant-bird gets hatched?"

I started to cry all over again.

"I'll be right there," Gail said, and hung up.

In the motel on Cape Cod this past Labor Day weekend, just two months ago, my father had woken me up in the middle of the night.

"She's in a lot of pain. We're going to drive back home so she can see Dr. Stone. Wake up, Neenie. We're leaving."

My father was whispering, but his voice sounded louder than usual. He was holding my shoulder too tight.

I opened my eyes. Only the bathroom light was on. No light came in through the curtains.

"What time is it?"

"Shh! I told you, your mother is in a lot of pain. Whisper!"

"What time is it?" I whispered.

"It's three in the morning. She's been in pain all night. Get dressed."

Her neck. Her neck still hurt.

"Where is she?" I whispered.

"She's in bed, but she's dressed and ready to go. She's lying down until we're all packed up." My father collected maps, books, socks as he whispered to me.

When his arms were full, he dumped everything into an open suitcase. It was a good thing my mother wasn't watching. Her head was under the covers.

I carried the suitcases outside. The air was soft and cool. The moon was high. The ocean smelled so calm, so peaceful. My mother appeared in the doorway, her eyes closed, leaning on my father's arm. She held her other arm across her eyes and hovered in the door for a moment. My father led her down the walk toward the car.

"It's so bright," she said. "It's so bright and so late."

She sat in the backseat. I put a pillow behind her head.

"Thanks, sweetie." She sighed.

"Do you want another one?" I asked.

"No, honey, this is fine," she said, and winced. Her eyes were still closed.

I climbed in the front, and my father got behind the wheel.

"Here we go," he said. "Keep your eyes closed, honey, and I'll get us home as fast as I can."

"Keep *your* eyes open," she said. "We don't need to go fast. Just safely."

My father started the car and backed out of the motel parking lot.

"Safely and as smoothly as possible," Mom said. "The bumps hurt like hell."

"Sorry," my father said.

My mother gasped softly every time we hit a bump in the road. There were about ten million bumps on the eight-hour drive from Cape Cod home to Roseville.

Gail ran up the stairs to my room, sat down next to me, and rubbed my back.

"I'm sorry," I said, weeping again. "I'm sorry. I didn't mean to do this. I just wanted to feel better. I didn't mean to do this."

"Who cares?" said Gail, rubbing my back more firmly. "Who gives a shit? Cry all you want."

"But I feel so dumb. I hate crying." I sobbed harder.

When my mother was home, after the first hospital, before the second, when we still didn't know what was wrong with her, she had spent hours crying. I never knew what to do when she cried. I should have known, I should have figured out how to make her feel better, but I didn't. I would stare at her, at the tears streaming down her cheeks, and wish I were a million miles away.

"It's so dumb. I feel so helpless. I wish there was something to do, something I could do, and there's not, there's nothing."

Gail hugged me, and I cried until I was limp, wrung out.

"I thought I was going crazy," I said. "I kept hearing all these books my mother used to read to me."

" 'I think I can, I think I can'?" Gail said, in Mrs. Redmond's voice.

"And ones I haven't thought about for years. *Caps for Sale?*"

"Tzt, tzt, tzt," Gail said, shaking her finger at me, just like the monkeys in the book. "You're regressing," she said. "Very appropriate."

I stared at her. Of course.

"I am, I am regressing. But there's no one to de-regress me." I burst into tears again.

" 'The Duke was six foot four and forty-six, and even colder than he thought he was,' " Gail quoted, rubbing my back again. Gail had loved listening to Mom read *The 13 Clocks.* "But the princess Saralinda escapes the castle, anyway."

"Where's my prince?" I wailed, and then burst into laughter.

"Where indeed?" Gail said.

Silence.

"Once, when I was little," I said, "I walked into the living room. My mother was sitting there reading a book and sobbing. I thought she was nuts. 'Are you crying about the book?' I asked her. 'Yes,' she sobbed. 'It's about a wonderful artist who is deformed. It's so sad.' "

"*Moulin Rouge?*" Gail asked.

"You are so literate," I said.

Silence.

"I couldn't understand how a book, printed words on a page, not even any pictures, how could that make you cry like a baby? And if it did, why would you keep reading it? The whole thing made no sense to me."

"And now you know," Gail said.

She sat with me, rubbing my back, both of us staring out my window.

"What time is it?" Gail asked suddenly. "I promised my mom I would feed Andrew."

"Oh."

"Come with me," she said. "He'd love to see you."

"Me, too," I said, and we walked over to Gail's.

Andrew was Gail's seven-year-old half brother. Gail's father had died when we were little, and her mother had remarried when we were eight. I loved Andrew.

When he was about two, Gail and I were in her room with the door closed. He had just learned to walk. He flung the door to Gail's room open, marched into the middle of her room, threw his arms wide open, grinned the most unbelievable grin, and yelled, "Hi!" He stood there, beaming, as if to say, "I know how glad you are to see me. I'm glad to see you, too. Isn't this just great?" He was completely certain that we would be as glad to see him as he was to see us.

Another time, he was toddling around the kitchen and he spotted a banana sitting on the table. He reached for it, held it in his chubby little hand, looked at me, put the banana to his ear, and said, "Hello!"

∾

Gail and I sat down at the dinner table with Andrew.

"Why do they call these things wings, anyway?" he asked Gail, holding up his chicken wing.

"What?"

"Why do they call these things wings?" Andrew repeated, still holding up his dinner.

"Because they are wings," said Gail. "They are chicken wings."

"Real chicken wings?" Andrew said, putting the wing back down on his plate.

"Yes," said Gail. "Real chicken wings."

"Real chicken wings from real chickens?" asked Andrew. "I'm eating a real live chicken?"

"No, it's not alive."

"I'm eating a real live dead chicken? A chicken that died? A chicken that used to be alive?"

"Yes," said Gail. "That's what chicken is."

"Oh, my God," said Andrew. "How could you feed me that yuck? Why didn't you tell me what I was eating?"

"I did tell you," Gail said. "I told you it was chicken."

"But you didn't tell me it was real chicken, like a real animal, you know what I mean." Andrew stared at his plate. "Mindy?"

"Yes, Andrew, it's true."

"What is broccoli, Mindy?" Andrew was still staring at his plate. "Did it used to be some kind of parrot?"

"No, you little goofball," I said. "Broccoli is a vegetable; it grows in the ground—or maybe on a broccoli tree or a broccoli vine. I don't know what it grows on, but it is a vegetable, and it grows out of the ground somehow."

"And mashed potatoes?" Andrew asked, still looking at his plate.

"They come from a box. See?" said Gail as she pointed to the big red mashed potato box on the counter.

"Potatoes are vegetables," I told Andrew. "They grow in the ground. They are tubers, and they grow in the ground by themselves. Not on a tree or a vine."

"Oh," said Andrew. "So everything on my plate was alive once and now it's dead."

"I guess you could say that," said Gail.

"Yuck! How does anyone eat after they know?" Andrew got up, pushed his chair away, and went upstairs. He slammed his door, the little brother I had always wanted, the little brother who would have made us a family, a family who talked, a real family.

I helped Gail clear. She washed, I dried in silence. Comfortable. It was so comfortable.

"They need to operate to remove the tumor," my father announced later that night. We were sitting in the living room, he with his feet up on his ottoman, arm casually draped on his side table, tapping his cigarette, me sitting on the love seat across from him. "They think it's about the size of a lemon. They'll remove as much of the tumor as they can," he was saying.

"What if they can't remove all of it?" I asked. What if they do remove all of the tumor and take her mind with it? Andrew would have asked that. I pulled my knees up and hugged them to my chest.

"I don't know. We will know more after the surgery. They can't tell anything until they operate."

Until they cut her head open. Say it! Say what you mean. Cut her head open.

"Then they test it to see if the tumor is malignant or not. They biopsy it," he said. "After that, we will know."

Biopsy. The word kept flashing on and off in my mind, like a neon sign. Biopsy.

"I have to go now," he said. "I want to see her tonight. Before the operation."

"Right," I said. The operation. The thing that happens before the biopsy.

"I'll see you tomorrow. Harry and Ben will pick you up in the morning and drive you to Syracuse. I'll meet you at the hospital." He patted my hand and went upstairs.

My father never talked. He announced. He proclaimed. And then he left.

"Now that you're in high school," he had said to me my first year, "we need to talk about dating."

Dating? No one had asked me for a date. What could he possibly have to legislate about dating? We had been sitting in the living room, in the same seats, me in the love seat, him in his chair and ottoman.

I waited.

"I cannot allow you to date anyone who isn't Jewish."

He could not allow me? Whose orders did he have to follow?

"That's it?" I asked.

"Yes. That's it," he said snidely, mocking me.

"Okay," I said.

We sat there, me staring at my feet, him tapping a cigarette and then lighting it.

I knew he wasn't through. I knew there was going to be more, and I couldn't get up. I couldn't allow myself to leave yet.

"The reason I am saying this now is that I want you to understand my position. I am forbidding you to date non-Jewish boys because I abhor and will not tolerate mixed marriage."

A bit more frankness than usual, I thought. Now he's forbidding me.

"Mixed marriage?" I asked. I knew what he meant, and he knew I knew.

"Your marrying a Gentile."

He used to call them *shagetzes*, or worse, use the correct plural, *shgutzim*. Made them sound like phlegm.

"Race," he continued, "is irrelevant. What I care about is the perpetuation of Judaism, of the Jewish religion, of the Jewish people. And I care about it very deeply. So deeply that I vow to you that were you to marry a non-Jew, I would sit shiva for you."

Silence.

"Really you would?" I asked finally. Would he?

"Yes. Don't test me, Neenie. Believe me. I would sit shiva for you, my only daughter, my only child, rather than condone the termination, the extermination of the Jewish race. I cannot condone that. I will not condone that. So I have no alternative but to say to you that should you condone it, should you do something to bring an end to the Jewish people, I would have to say the prayer for the dead for you and act from then on as if you were dead. You would be dead to me."

That was the end of the conversation. I knew that. We stared at each other.

"Okay," I said. "I understand."

"No, of course I wouldn't," my mother had said when I asked her if she would sit shiva for me. "Never."

"And Daddy really would, wouldn't he?"

"He might," she had whispered. "But I never would." And she hugged me and repeated, "Never."

I heard the back door slam. I heard my father rev his car and drive off. And then there was silence. Except inside my head, where the word *biopsy* bonged all too loudly.

I had a million questions, but none my father wanted to hear. Did Mom know she had a brain tumor? Did she know her brain was going to be opened up? Was she scared? Was she in pain? Oh, God, was she in real pain? I had thought the wincing was all drama, but it was real, it was true, and I hadn't believed her. I was a monster.

I stared at the candy bowl that sat on the coffee table, a china bowl, decorated with Chinese scrolls, sitting on funny-looking black clawed feet. The top had a black, pointy handle. It was always full of M&M's. Every time I opened it, for as long as I could remember, it was full to the brim. I never thought about how it stayed that way. I'd take a handful and throw them in my mouth all together. No matter how many handfuls I gobbled down, the dish was always full. I lifted the top now. There were a few M&M's at the bottom. I had never seen the bottom of the dish before. It was white. I closed the top. Of course the dish was empty. My mother was the only one who filled it.

I went upstairs to my room and sat on my bed, staring at nothing. Then I noticed a hair on my leg that looked funny, different from the others. I had started shaving my legs the year before. I loved the silky way they felt just after I shaved. But this hair was odd, bigger than the others, almost bushy. I went to my mother's bathroom and took her tweezers out of the medicine cabinet. Every so often she would have my father pull little hairs out of her chin, hairs she couldn't see herself. I went back to my room and pulled the bushy hair. It didn't hurt as much as I thought it would. The thing about it was that even though the hair was very thick, its follicle was tiny, a tiny black dot. I pulled out the hair next to it, a regular-looking hair, thin compared to the first. But this one had an enormous root, almost like the tattletails Mrs. Piggle-Wiggle made appear on the ceiling when her kids told fibs. This was really interesting. You couldn't tell what kind of root you would pull up by looking at the kind of hair it produced. I pulled up a lot before I realized it was getting late and I should go to sleep.

I got into bed, closed my eyes, and saw a lemon inside my mother's head. Why a lemon? In *Death Be Not Proud,* the doctors told John Gunther that his son's brain tumor was the size of an orange. My mother's was smaller. That must be good. That must be better than John Gunther's poor son. I saw lemons and oranges lining up on a basketball court, ready to take each other on. The ball was a kumquat. The lemons were winning. They were smaller and faster. The lemons were winning by a mile.

# CHAPTER THREE

*Monday*
*November 6, 1961*

THE DOCTOR HAD AN ADAM's apple that looked more like an elbow poking through his neck. I watched it ride up and down as he spoke.

"We removed the whole tumor, every bit of it," he said. "That is very good. I am pleased about that. But it was bigger than we thought. As big as a grapefruit." He made a ball shape with his hands.

A grapefruit? No, it couldn't be that big. It wouldn't fit inside her head. It was a lemon before, what happened to the lemon?

"Now we just have to wait for the results of the biopsy." The doctor was still talking. "Then we will know more."

"How is she, how is my mom?" I asked. He kept talking as if all we cared about was the tumor, not the woman the tumor was attached to. Why didn't he operate on his own Adam's apple? It was as big as a lemon.

"She's resting quietly," he said, patting me on the shoulder.

"How long will the biopsy take?" my father asked.

Didn't anyone want to know about my mother?

"Is she still in pain? Does her neck still hurt her so much?" My father put his hand on my arm to stop me, but I ignored him.

"Does she hurt?"

"No, she is asleep, and she is quite comfortable," the doctor said.

How did he know she was comfortable? What did he know about comfort? He couldn't be comfortable, with that elbow sticking out of his throat.

"We will know more when the biopsy results come back," he said, and patted me again. "It should take about a week. Then we'll talk again."

"Does she know?" I asked, shutting my eyes, leaning against the door on my side of the car. We were almost home.

"Hmm?" asked my father.

"Does she know? Mommy. Does she know?"

"Know?" he asked.

"Know she has a brain tumor?" I blurted out, and opened my eyes.

He pulled a cigarette out of his breast pocket, tapped it on the dashboard, put it in his mouth, and pushed in the cigarette lighter. He pushed it hard.

"Does she know?" I asked again. "Does she know what's wrong with her? That she had an operation on her brain?"

"No," he said.

"What does she think?"

"Before the operation she thought she was having more tests. The doctors didn't want to scare her. They advised against telling her anything until we knew more."

The lighter popped. My father lit his cigarette.

She knows, I thought. She knows everything. She always knew when I was faking being sick so I didn't have to go to school. She always knew when I had ruined my appetite by eating M&M's before dinner. When she's better, she'll explain how she knew everything, and we'll laugh at the stupid doctors who thought they could trick her. We'll laugh our heads off when that stupid biopsy comes back negative. We'll laugh about being worried, about thinking she might die. We'll laugh about all of it, and then we'll go eat ice cream.

When my mother was home, between hospitals, when they knew she didn't have spinal meningitis but they still didn't know what she did have, my father had given her a bell to ring whenever she needed anything. It was a dinner bell, a glass thing with a tall handle. My mother used it to call me.

She rang. I went in.

"Hi, sweetie," she said. She was sitting up in bed, resting against the bed pillow.

"Do you need something?" I asked, trying not to sound as impatient as I felt.

"I just wanted to tell you that I love you."

"I know, Mom." I turned to go.

"Do you think that man still thinks we're following him?" she asked me.

I turned back and smiled.

"I wonder if he remembers us at all," she said, almost to herself. "Strange, isn't it? He has become one of us, and he doesn't even know."

I stood there, waiting for her to finish.

"I love you," she said.

"I know. I have to finish my homework. I have a lot."

"Go ahead, honey. I love you. Madame Lebrun and her daughter."

I left.

She rang again. I went back.

"Put on my Julie Andrews record, sweetie." She smiled faintly. "Her voice sounds like a bell."

I put on *Camelot.*

"What a beautiful voice. It makes me cry."

She hummed along and cried, hummed and cried.

"Mindy, I love you. I only hope whatever I have is not hereditary. I love you so much."

What did she think she had that I could inherit?

She closed her eyes. I watched her for a few minutes, to make sure she was asleep before I turned off the record player.

Suddenly she sat bolt upright, her eyes wild, and screamed, "River! Stay away from my door!"

She sat like that, her eyes wide, her arms raised to hold off the river. Then she lay back down, her eyes closed, and she slept.

I stood by the door, staring. Maybe she hadn't just screamed. Maybe I had imagined it. She seemed so sound asleep now. "River, stay away from my door"? What river? What door? I kept staring at her, but she was really asleep.

ॐ

When we got home after the surgery, my father went to his room and I went to mine. I hated this time of day—twilight. The gray time, the time I had to rush home to an empty house. It was especially gray and bleak now, in Roseville, in November. I sat on my bed, staring out the window at my cherry tree.

I used to climb my cherry tree and sit there forever. In the winter I sat bundled up in my leggings and jacket, clinging to the icy branches until I thought my arms and legs would freeze. In the spring I would sit surrounded by white blossoms, at one with my tree. But the summer was best. The leaves were thick and dark green, and there were bright red cherries growing everywhere. My mother would make cherry pie from my tree's cherries. Oh, I had been so mad at her for that. I had refused to eat it. Looking at the pie revolted me.

I went to my desk to start my homework. What was my homework? I had missed school today. I could call Gail and find out. But I didn't. I started a letter to my mother. I would give it to my father to give her. What should I say? She didn't even know she had a brain tumor. She must know they operated on her head, but what had they told her? I had to write about me, only about me.

*Dear Mom,*

*Gail loaned me her paperback copy of* Peyton Place *and I'm reading it. School is the same old thing except we got a new kid in our English class. His name is Bobby. He is about six feet tall, skinny, and dresses like a hood, all in black. He's from New York City and he's not Jewish. (Don't tell Dad that part.)*

Here I was writing things to my mother that I never would have said to her if she'd been home. I never talked to her about boys, and I never would have told her about *Peyton Place.*

*He looks like an Italian version of Abraham Lincoln, but cuter. Remember when I was eight and I had a crush on Lincoln? Maybe I never told you. It was when Daddy bought the* World Book Encyclopedia. *I read the biography of Lincoln in the encyclopedia over and over. I used to imagine I lived back then in a cabin right near Abe's, and he and I walked to school together, and he was very shy but he was really madly in love with me and we picked blueberries in the woods one day and he kissed me just as my bucket got full of berries and he tipped the berries over and we had to start picking all over again.*

I couldn't send this letter. My mother would think I had gone crazy. I started again.

*Dear Mom,*

*Don't worry. I'm doing my homework every night and I get a hamburger at McDonald's or go to Gail's for dinner, or I fry myself some eggs, easy over, with toast and jelly. I am getting very good at frying eggs. I can also make a mean peanut butter and jelly sandwich.*

*I sent away for all my college applications, so I will start writing them next week when they arrive. Gail is finished with hers. I'll bring mine with me when I come to see you so you can help me edit the essay.*

*I love you and miss you. See you soon.*

*Love,*

*Mindy*

I hadn't sent away for the applications yet. I had filled out the postcards, but I hadn't mailed them. I didn't want to lie to my mother anymore, not when she was so helpless. I would give my father the letter once I mailed the postcards. I folded the letter and stuck it in my pocketbook. I had been so mean to her before the first hospital, not believing that she was really sick. I thought she was being a big baby, complaining about every bump in the road, acting like she was in so much pain that we had to travel in the middle of the night to get her home from Cape Cod to see her doctor. And I had refused to see *Spartacus* with her that last night in Cape Cod.

"Honey, look," my father had said that night, "*Spartacus* is playing. It's right down the road, and it starts in a half hour."

"Perfect," my mother said, rubbing her neck. "I've been dying to see it."

"I haven't been dying to see it," I said. "I don't want to see it. I hate blood-and-guts movies."

"It's about freedom, Mindy," my mother said. "About a slave's fight for freedom against oppression."

"I don't care. It's all going to be blood-and-guts, anyway. Boring. I'd rather stay home and read."

Which is what I did. At first I opened the door to the balcony so I could hear the wind and smell the ocean. The wind was really whipping up. I stared at the ocean for a while. It was so vast and so cold and bleak. The wind swirled through the beach grass. It was beautiful—solemnly, dramatically, starkly beautiful. I couldn't look for too long. I came back inside to finish *The Old Man and the Sea*.

I had to apologize to her. What would I say? I'm sorry, Mama. I didn't realize you had a brain tumor. I just thought you had a little pain in the neck, that you were exaggerating. I'm so sorry. Get sick as much as you want, complain about it all you want. Just come home from the hospital. Come home and we can fight again, but from now on I won't mean it.

I looked through my mother's old record collection. When I was little, she used to play me these records and sing along with them. When I got my own hi-fi last year, she let me keep them in my room. I put on her favorite: "Accentuate the Positive." "Eliminate the negative and latch on to the affirmative," I sang along. And then "Mairzy Doats." "A kiddley divey too, wouldn't you?"

How sick was she? Could she think? Was her head completely shaved now?

Was she going to die?

# CHAPTER FOUR

*Friday*
*November 10, 1961*

AFTER SCHOOL I DROVE to the library to start on my senior thesis. Education. I would do it on something
about education. I went to the big card catalog and
stared at the cards under "Education." Then I went to
the *L*s and looked up "Lebrun." I had never seen that
painting. Had my mother ever seen it? Why had she
loved it so much? Élisabeth Louise Vigeé-Lebrun
(1753–1842). A book called *Masterpieces in Colour.* I
found the book, and then I found the painting. I knew
it was the one the moment I saw it. The mother encir-
cled her daughter in her arms, the daughter's arms
were around her mother's neck, and they both gazed
out of the painting, comfortable, so comfortable, so at
peace in each other's arms. So beautiful. I closed the
book and reshelved it.

∽

Gert, our next-door neighbor, saw me drive in and came over.

"How is your mother?" she asked, lowering her voice, like everyone did when they asked about her.

"She's resting comfortably. The doctor said he got it all out. Now we just have to wait for the biopsy," I whispered back. The three sentences flowed effortlessly. Monkey see, monkey do. Follow the bouncing Adam's apple. Trying to sound like I knew what I was talking about, like I wasn't in the middle of some horrible nightmare where nothing made sense, like a soupy fog hadn't fallen across the world. "The doctor is pleased."

"Good," she said. "Good."

Good? How could any of this be good? If this is good, then what is bad?

"If God is God He is not good, / If God is good He is not God; / Take the even, take the odd." My father used to quote Archibald MacLeish. Why? I couldn't remember. Some play, some play about Job. My mother never read stuff like that. The two books she had on her nightstand ever since I could remember were Dr. Spock and *Fight Against Fears*, which had the oddest cover: a naked woman, crouched, her head bent down to her knees, her face covered by her hands. She looked like she was crying, but she was in such a precarious position; she might tip over at any moment. How could you

42

cry that way? Maybe she hadn't been crying, just hiding. It was always a puzzle to me, the cover of that book. And naked? Why was she naked? All I remembered about Dr. Spock was that it was pink and blue. Could she read now?

"And your dad?" Gert asked.

"He's okay."

"I hardly see him. Is he ever home?"

"No. He drives to Syracuse after work every night, stays in a motel so he can see my mom in the morning, and then he drives back to work. Sometimes he stops home before he drives to Syracuse in the evening. But mostly not. He sees her every day. And still goes to the office six days a week."

Silence.

"Come over for dinner whenever you want," Gert said. "Or just come over. Anytime." She hugged me.

"Thanks."

ॐ

While we waited for the biopsy, I drove my mother's car every day after school. I drove out Steuben Street and kept going until I was in farmland, beautiful rolling hills, barns, silos, white churches with steeples. The road weaved around, and the hills were short and steep. The trees were bare. Andrew used to

43

call them bald. I drove and drove, the radio blasting, my mind a total blank. There were just bald trees, winding roads, me and the music. It was good, it was good to move, to drive, to be blank.

I had always loved driving. When I was fourteen, my parents let me drive in the driveway. Not on the street until it was legal, until I was sixteen. I drove every day after school. Our driveway was connected to Gert's, so I drove from Beaumont Circle to Parkview Drive. Back and forth, forward and then reverse. In the winter, when there were big piles of snow on either side of the driveway, I practiced driving into the snow-banks, getting stuck, and rocking the car forward and back to get unstuck. You could only do that with a manual transmission. First gear, then reverse, then first, then reverse, until the car had some momentum, and then you gunned it and leaped out of the snowbank.

But now I could drive on the street. I drove to Paris, Poland, Russia. I followed roads to every oddly named town I could find. It was me and my mother's Plymouth. The car was painted what she called robin's-egg blue, and it had push-button driving. My father's cars always had manual transmissions. I had learned to drive on his car, practicing shifting gears while I waited alone in the car for him to run errands. My mother's car was an automatic, a word my father said with a sneer, the same tone he used when he said guitars were not real instruments because they had frets. So here I was, finally, with an easy-to-use piece of equipment. I loved it. Push a button, you're in drive. Once in drive, stay in drive until you need the brake. That's it. Steer, drive, and brake, no worrying about stalling or being in neutral by mistake. This was easy. This was living.

I watched the sky to see how much longer I could keep driving. I had a junior license. I couldn't drive after dark. I timed it pretty well, driving into the driveway while I could still see without turning on the headlights. I parked the car in the garage in my mother's space. My father's space was empty. The house was dark. I walked through the back door, as I always did. But there were no lights on. And there were no smells. It was warm inside, but dark and empty. I turned on the light in the kitchen. The bowl I had eaten my cereal in still sat on the kitchen table, the spoon still in the bowl, the little bit of milk and soggy cornflakes still there. My mother always cleaned up the kitchen. She never even left dishes in the sink.

The window seat in the front hall was empty. I stared at it. My mother always sat on the window seat to sort the mail into piles—one for her, one for my father, one for me. She left my father's and my piles on the seat. I looked on the floor in front of the door,

where the mail came in through the slot. A jumble of
mail lay there. Some was still stuck through the slot,
hanging like a big white tongue. I pulled all the mail
together and sat on the window seat, sorting it into
piles. My father's pile was always biggest. It was today.
Nothing for me. Whose pile got the ones addressed to
Occupant, I wondered.

I went upstairs. My bed was still unmade, just the
way I had left it that morning. But my bed was never
unmade. Every day of my life when I came home from
school, I came home to a tightly tucked bed, the white
chenille bedspread flat and unwrinkled, the pillows
fluffed up at the head. I put my books on the floor and
plunked down on my unmade bed. A stranger in my
strange house. It was deafeningly quiet.

MinDEEE. My mother would yell my name. She
accented the last syllable. She did the same when she
called my father—LeoNERD. She accented the NERD
and raised the pitch of her voice so it almost sounded
like the beginning of an aria. The housewife soprano.

I turned on the radio in my room full blast so I
could hear it wherever I went. I turned on all the lights
in every room I walked through, but the house still
didn't feel right. "Keep away from Runaround Sue."

"Dr. Stone called," my father had announced only
a month ago. "He wants to send your mother to a

hospital in Syracuse. A bigger hospital where they have better facilities and where they can find out what is wrong with her."

"What do they think is wrong with her?" I asked.

"He doesn't know. That's why he wants to send her to Syracuse, to do tests and find out."

"What kind of tests?" I was the one who kept taking tests—SATs, the Regents exam.

"I don't *know*, Neenie." His mouth was getting smaller and smaller. "I told you everything Dr. Stone told me."

"Oh," I said.

I had stopped myself from asking anything more. He wouldn't answer. His mouth would just keep getting smaller until it was a tiny pinhole. And then he would hum.

"They will take her in an ambulance tomorrow morning. I'll go with her. You can visit on the weekend. You don't need to miss school."

"She'll be there that long?"

"Probably. Yes, I think so. Probably."

"Oh."

"If she's not there, then she'll be home and you can see her here."

"Oh."

When I was six, we visited my mother's parents in

Florida, and my mother took me to a riding stable. I fell in love with riding and with the beautiful palomino I rode every day, Buttermilk. My mother used to sing "Ole Buttermilk Sky" to me on the way to the stable.

When we were on the train returning home, I asked my father if I could have my own horse.

"Sure." He smiled. "When you're ten, you can have one."

"Really? A horse of my very own?"

"Yes," he said. "If you still want one when you're ten, you can have one."

The day before my tenth birthday, I said, "So this is the year I get my horse, Dad."

"What?"

I repeated myself.

"What horse?"

What horse? He must be joking. I looked into his eyes, and I couldn't tell.

"The horse you promised me when we were in Florida and I rode Buttermilk every day and I asked you if I could have a horse of my own and you said yes I could when I was ten and tomorrow I'm ten."

He looked at me blankly.

"Don't you remember? We were on the train coming home, we were eating in the dining car?"

"I don't know what you're talking about, Neenie."

He laughed, patted my head, and picked up his newspaper.

But I knew. I knew he had promised. And I was almost sure he knew, too—

The phone rang. It was Gail.

"How is your mother?" she asked.

"We're waiting," I said. I pulled the phone into my room and turned down the radio.

"Still? For the biopsy?"

"Yes."

"Are you okay?"

"Yes," I lied. I sat down on my bed.

"Sure?"

"I *used* to be Shoor," my mother would say. Another one of her expressions. Shoor had been her maiden name.

"Yes."

Silence.

"Switch of gears?" she asked.

"Please."

"You have to make me a promise," she said. "You have to promise that you will do this."

"What? Promise that I will do what?" I twirled the phone cord around my thumb.

"Promise that you will do this when I tell you I am getting married."

"Married? You? To who?"

"No. I'm serious."

"Then act serious. Just tell me what you want me to do and then I'll tell you whether or not I'll do it."

"Okay. I guess I got a little carried away."

"I guess. So now take a deep breath. Don't say anything. Breathe." I heard some noise at the other end of the line. "Okay. Now speak. Slowly." I untwirled the cord.

"Okay. I want you to send me a milk glass orange juice squeezer when I tell you that I am about to get married."

"That's it? A milk glass orange juice squeezer?" I dropped the phone cord and watched it wriggle on the floor.

"Yes. And I promise to do the same for you."

"Great. Thanks a lot. Why do I want a milk glass orange juice squeezer? And what is milk glass? Won't it make the orange juice curdle?"

"I just read a story about a girl who was all happy about how great it was to get married and then she started to open her wedding presents and she was still giddy and thrilled and then she opened this milk glass orange juice squeezer and it made her realize that she was miserable and she didn't want to get married and she really hated the guy." Gail stopped talking. I stuck my foot in the cord and wound it up my calf.

"So I want you to promise that if I ever get myself into a situation like that, you know, all breathless with what I am supposed to be feeling, that you will give me the chance to come down to earth and figure out what I really feel like. Get it?"

"A milk glass orange juice squeezer?"

"That's what it was in the story."

"Does it have to be milk glass? What if I can't find a milk glass one? What if I have to order it and it doesn't get here in time and you get married and when you come back from your honeymoon there it is waiting for you and you open it and you realize that you hate the guy—he is a killer—but it's too late." I pushed the cord off my calf with my other toe.

"Well, don't send it too late. Either get it on time or forget it. No. Don't just forget it. I couldn't live like that. No, send me any old orange juice squeezer. But try to get a milk glass one. Really try. Okay?"

"Okay." I struggled to pick up the cord with my toes.

"Maybe we should try and find them now and then save them for each other. But then again we'd probably lose them. I don't really want to take a squeezer to college. Okay. We'll just have to try and find them then. And if we can't, we'll make do."

Pause.

"The funny thing is that it was such a stupid story. Not well written. But the squeezer really got to me."

"It certainly did," I said. I lay down on my bed on my back.

We were both silent for a while, comfortably silent, as if we were sitting next to each other at the movies. My mother and her biopsy felt far away.

"How's *Peyton Place*?" Gail asked me. "Like it?"

"The dirty stuff is cool," I said. "But the rest is so boring. Good rich people, bad rich people, good poor people, bad poor people. And the descriptions. They go on and on—enough with the Indian summer as sexpot. Did you really finish it?" I rolled over and walked to the window.

"No. I just skimmed through it to make sure I read all the dirty parts. They're real short. Easy to miss."

"That's a relief," I said. "I thought you finished it and I was missing out on some truly great literary something."

"No," said Gail. "Just truly great smut. Well, just smut."

Silence.

"My mom's calling. Gotta go. See ya tomorrow. Bye." She hung up.

I hung up, put the phone on the floor, and stared at my cherry tree. I could barely see it in the darkness.

My mother had told me last year that I should read *Lady Chatterley's Lover.* "A beautiful love story," she called it. "The most beautiful love story you will ever read."

I had stared at her. "Ma, it's a dirty book," I blurted out.

"People say that. People who don't understand beauty. Read it yourself. You'll see."

I had never opened the book.

*Friday*
*November 17, 1961*

"It was malignant," my father said.

That means she's going to die, I thought. That's what malignant means. Why doesn't he say, Your mother is going to die? Why does he say her tumor is malignant? Why doesn't he ever say what he means? Why is the room getting dim?

"The doctor says they will start X-ray treatments

this week. They moved her to a new room on a different floor, nearer to the X-ray center."

"Oh," I said.

Silence.

"So we'll see how the treatments go?" I asked.

"Yes."

Silence.

"Are you okay?" my father asked me.

"Yeah, sure," I said.

"It's not that much of a shock, is it? You did know this was more than likely, didn't you?"

"Yes," I said. "I knew."

But I didn't know.

"So now we have to wait and see how the X-ray treatments go?" I asked again.

"Yes," he said.

"How long?" I asked.

"How long for what?"

"How long do we wait to see if they work?"

"I don't know," he said.

We sat silently.

"She doesn't recognize anyone, but I think she knows I'm there. I hold her hand, and sometimes she cries. The doctor said no one really knows what she can hear or see. I know she'd like to see you."

What? What are you talking about?

"Neenie?"

"She doesn't recognize anyone?" I whispered.

"No, honey, of course not," he said.

"Since when? Since when hasn't she recognized anyone? Since when don't they know what she can hear or see? Since when?" My voice was getting too loud. "Since when?" I whispered.

"Neenie. What do you mean? Why, since the operation, of course."

"You mean you have gone to visit her every night and you don't know if she knows you are there?"

"Yes."

"Why didn't you tell me? Why didn't you tell me she was like that all this time?" I was whispering again.

"Neenie, I thought you knew. She had a brain tumor, honey, the size of a grapefruit. Of course she would be like that." My father sat stiffly in his big old chair. He wore his "I only want the best for you, dear" look.

"I just read a whole book about a brain tumor. John Gunther's son wasn't like that. He was writing letters to Albert Einstein, for God's sake. He was doing homework, he was telling his father to keep writing his book, he was having friends from school visit him. How would I know?"

I had never thought she would be like that. I had

only thought she might die. When we had been walking up the hospital's marble steps, the second hospital,
the day of the operation, I had thought, When this is all
over, we'll all laugh about it, how Daddy and I waited
for the doctor to tell us the results of the operation, and
then I almost tripped because the thought that came
barreling into my head was, When this is all over,
you might never laugh about it at all. She might
be dead. But I had never thought she wouldn't
know me.

"I'm sorry, Neenie. I just thought you did know."

"Well, I didn't!"

Silence.

"How long will she not know anybody?" I asked.

"How long?"

"Yes." My voice was getting louder again. I pulled
my legs up and hugged them. "What did the doctor say
about when this would change?" I whispered.

Silence.

"They haven't said anything about that," my father
said. Cigarette smoke whirled up around his head. He
breathed deeply.

Silence.

"Do you want to see her?" He tapped his ashes casually into the ashtray.

See her? Who was she now? Who would I see?

"I don't know. I don't know. I need to think."

"Okay," he said. "Think about it. I think it might be a good idea."

"Okay, I'll think about it."

But I wouldn't. I wouldn't think about it. I wouldn't think about visiting someone who used to be my mother, who couldn't recognize me anymore.

"I wrote her a letter," I whispered.

"What?" Smoke whirled again.

"Nothing. I have homework. I'm going upstairs."

"I'll call you tomorrow," he said, and crushed his cigarette out in the ashtray.

I sat on my bed and listened to my father's car drive off.

When I was about eleven, my father asked me who I wanted to live with if he and my mother both died at the same time.

"How could you both be dead?"

"It will never happen, honey," my father said in his oily, sweet voice. "It's just a what-if. We have to write something down for a what-if. It won't ever happen."

"I want to live with Gail," I said. That would be fun. I'd have Gail *and* Andrew.

"No, honey, you have to pick a relative. That's the way it's done. You'll live with your aunt Fanny."

"Okay," I said. Why had he asked if I didn't have a choice?

He must be wrong. The biopsy must be wrong. But my father had said she didn't speak, she didn't recognize him. So it was like she was dead, anyway. But he went to visit her every day. How could he not have told me? How could I not have known all this time? What has he been doing there every day? Sitting in the room with a dead person?

What was I going to do? I couldn't sit here. I had to move. It was dark. I couldn't drive. I didn't want to talk to anyone. I didn't want to think. She was going to die. She wouldn't be here when I got home from school every day, when I came home from college, when I went to college. She wasn't even really here now. How could this happen? My life had been so normal, so uninteresting, so run-of-the-mill. This couldn't be happening to me. Please, please, let my mind go blank, let me not be able to think. This is temporary. This is only temporary. Why doesn't he ask the doctors how long the treatments will take?

I put on my coat and ran outside. I couldn't drive. I couldn't break the law, even now. I would walk. That would have to do. It was cold out. That was good. No one was around. I walked down to Onondaga Street. There were cars there, but no pedestrians. No one would notice me. I could pretend I was invisible. Count the leaves on the ground. So many of them, dark beneath the streetlights. All of them dead. Count the dead leaves.

Don't leave me, Mama. Please, please.

How long did she have? I had to see her. I had to try and talk to her. Surely she would recognize me, her only child. Of course she would. I would go sit there and read her the letter I wrote her and talk to her and squeeze her hand, and she would squeeze back and smile and say she loved me. And I would say I loved her. And she would get better.

She would squeeze my hand when I was little. That meant she loved me. It was a signal only the two of us knew. We would be walking along, anywhere, and one of us would squeeze the other's hand, and we each knew. We knew that we loved each other. Sometimes we looked at each other and sometimes we just squeezed, without looking. My favorite times were when we didn't look. We just squeezed. One, two, three. That meant "I love you." No one else could tell that we were squeezing. We just looked like a mother and daughter walking down the street, holding hands. But we knew. It was our secret.

And the X-ray treatments! They will do X-ray treatments and the X-rays will melt the tumor away.

Me and X-ray treatments. We would save her. I turned around and started to walk back home. I breathed deeply. I must have been holding my breath before. I walked home fast, kicking the leaves around.

ℭ

The next morning I got in my mother's car and drove to Syracuse. It didn't matter that my parents didn't let me drive on the highway. I was a good driver. I knew the Thruway. I could do it. And I would be back way before dark.

I went to the front desk at the hospital and found out my mother's new room number. I took the elevator up and walked down the hall until I found her. There was a tiny, skinny person all in white sitting up in a big white bed, propped up with lots of pillows. I looked at the name on the chart on the door. It was my mother's name. But this woman was not my mother. Her eyes just stared off at the wall across the room. She had some bandages on her head, and where the bandages didn't cover, she had no hair. She was thinner than she had ever been, and it wasn't that she cried; it was that tears streamed out of her eyes but you couldn't really call it crying. Her eyes were leaking. I sat in a slippery red chair that was next to the head of her bed. I took her hand in mine. She stared at the wall across the room. I held her hand, but she didn't hold mine back. I squeezed her hand ever so lightly. I was afraid to jiggle anything about her frail body. Her hand just lay there in mine. I was holding hands with a ghost who didn't recognize me, who didn't even feel me. The room was so quiet. Empty. I was alone in this room, holding something in my hand, something that had no feeling, no weight, no give-and-take. This person didn't smell like my mother. She didn't smell at all.

Maybe it would take a few minutes, I thought.

I sat there with her hand in mine, watching her look at the wall, wetness dripping from her eyes.

"It's me, Mama," I whispered. "Your sweetie." I squeezed her hand again.

She stared at the wall.

I let go of her hand, opened my pocketbook, and took out the letter I had written her. I unfolded the letter. Read it out loud, I thought. Why? She can't hear anything. She doesn't even know I'm here. I took her hand again, squeezed it, and read the letter to myself. She stared at the wall across the room.

"Mama, it's me," I whispered again, and squeezed three times. "I love you, remember? Three times means 'I love you.' "

She stared at the wall. Her hand lay limp in mine.

Try reading out loud. Try. I read the letter out loud, softly, looking up at her, the way she used to read to me. She stared at the wall.

I closed my eyes and pictured my mother, my real mother, the mother who sang show tunes off-key while she made me a grilled cheese sandwich, the mother who took me to her younger brother's grave and told me stories about him, about my uncle Irving who she adored, who died before I was born, the mother who taught me how to diagram sentences, the mother who read me Dr. Seuss books over and over, the mother who "used to be Shoor," who said, "That's what makes horse races," and "At home we have it with whipped cream and nuts."

I opened my eyes. This woman whose hand I was holding was still staring at the wall, oblivious, her eyes still leaking. I took a tissue and gently wiped her cheeks dry. She stared at the wall. She hadn't even noticed my touch. I closed my eyes again. Maybe if I just sit here, sit here and hold her hand, sit still and just breathe, just be near her, she will wake up, she will shake her head and say, "Hi, sweetie."

My father and I used to watch my mother fall asleep on the train to Florida to visit my grandparents. Her head would drop down, bob up, drop down halfway, bob up, drop down. We used to watch her and bet on how many bobs she would make until her head finally rested on her chest.

I sat with my eyes closed. Then I opened them and looked around the room. The room was as vacant as this woman. No flowers, no pictures. White walls. White window shades. White blanket. White sheet. White woman.

Did the hospital move all the pictures out of this room and put them in rooms where patients could see them? I closed my eyes. Why didn't my father bring flowers? Why didn't he bring her Jean Naté? Why didn't he bring her pictures, the ones she had on her desk of a beaming Uncle Irving, posing next to the six-foot sailfish he had caught, and the one she had of me, age six, grinning from the top of my cherry tree, dressed in my navy blue dotted swiss dress with the hoop crinoline? How could he come here every day and look at the whiteness?

I put her hand down on the bed very gently and patted it. And then I ran out of the room and down the stairs to the car.

# CHAPTER FIVE

NOW I HAD TO DRIVE home. At least that gave me something to do, something to do so I didn't have to think. I started the car and drove. I found the Thruway entrance, and then I didn't even have to think about the direction. It was straight on until the next exit. I turned the radio way up.

I just drove. When a great song came on, I sang along with it, real loud. I kept my mind blank, completely blank. Then I saw the sign that said HERKIMER 5 MILES. I had passed my exit. I got off at the next one, crossed over the highway, and got back on again. I concentrated hard and didn't drive by the exit this time. I didn't know where to go. I couldn't go home. I couldn't look at our house, my mother's house. Not yet.

How could she? How could she forget me? How could she do this to me?

I drove around town, back and forth through neighborhoods where I didn't know anyone. I wanted to keep moving. So I drove around and around and finally drove to Gail's. I parked in front of her house and went in.

"Mindy!" yelled Andrew, running down the stairs into my arms. I scooped him up.

"Is she dead?" he asked, eye to eye with me. "Your mom. Is she dead?"

Gail's mother shrieked, "Andrew!"

Andrew's eyes held mine.

"No," I said. "She's not dead." Not literally.

Andrew threw his arms around my neck and squeezed. It felt great.

"Yippee ganippee!" he yelled.

I laughed.

He hopped down and ran up the stairs. "Come see my homework. I did it all myself," he yelled back down. And then he yelled really loud, "Yea! Mindy's mom's not dead!"

"How is she, Mindy?" asked Gail's mother.

"She's resting comfortably. The doctor said he got it all out. Now we just have to wait for the biopsy." The three sentences still flowed effortlessly.

"Good," she said. "Good. Gail's upstairs in her room. Sorry about Andrew."

"Don't be," I said. "It's such a relief to hear some-one say what they really mean."

She smiled at me and patted my shoulder.

I ran upstairs. Why was I *still* saying we were waiting for the biopsy? The tears started before I got to Gail's room. I opened her door. She was sketching. She looked up.

"What's the matter?" she asked. She put the charcoal down. "What's the matter?"

I stood in the doorway. She came to me, put her arm around my shoulder, and led me to the chair. I fell into it. Gail pulled my coat off and left it lying across the back of the chair.

"I just came back from Syracuse," I whispered. "I saw her."

Silence.

"She's not there," I said.

"What do you mean? They moved her?"

"No, no. She's not here. She's not in her body. She has left her body. It's like she's dead." I stared at Gail. She stared back. She took my hand in hers, and I sobbed. She held my hand, and I cried and cried. "It was so awful. My father told me last night. But I didn't believe him. I went to make her better. But I can't. She's gone. I can't do anything. It's too late. It's not fair. I didn't get a chance. I didn't have time. I wanted to. I really wanted to."

Gail rubbed my back and said, "It's okay. It's okay."

"It's not okay. It will never be okay. It's the most un-okay thing that has ever happened to me." I kept sobbing and she kept patting.

"You're right," she said.

"After my grandfather died, my uncle Sidney said that death was not God's punishment for the dead person but for someone else, someone still living."

"Is that what you believe?"

"I've always thought about it, after that. Every time a person I knew died, I wondered, Is this one my fault? But now it's my mother. Now I know. This one is my fault. This is completely my fault."

Gail hugged me tight. "It's nobody's fault," she said. "Nobody's."

"No," I sobbed. "It has to be somebody's. I want to blame her. I want to blame her for getting sick, for deserting me. But I can't."

Gail hugged and patted. "God's will," she whispered. "Sometimes we can't understand."

I sobbed, "Doesn't it bother you that sometimes He is so mean? And not fair. Not fair at all. Life is supposed to be fair. It was always supposed to be. Didn't you always believe that? The righteous shall inherit the earth; the good guys always win. I was raised on that. And it's not true. It's not true."

"Nothing you ever did was bad enough to deserve

this," Gail said. "And nothing your mother ever did was bad enough either."

Oh, my God. I stared at Gail. I wasn't thinking of Mom. I had been thinking only of me.

"You're right. She is the one who's dying." I burst into new tears. I thought I had dried up, but here was a whole new well, a well of tears for her, for my mother, for her dying. I had been thinking only of me, of her leaving me. But she was leaving, too; she was leaving her life.

Gail pulled me up and got me to lie down on her guest twin bed. She covered me with her quilt and got a cold washcloth to put on my forehead. I just kept crying and crying. And then I turned away and fell asleep, with Gail patting my back.

∾

I opened my eyes. Gail was sitting at her desk sketching. Everything seemed blurry, foggy. I rubbed my eyes. Everything was still blurry. Like a fog had descended, like the early-morning fog we drove through on the way back from the Cape.

"Is it foggy in here?" I asked her.

"No," she said.

"I can't see very well."

"Maybe you need some more sleep."

I thought about that and decided she was wrong.

"No. I think I need to tell you exactly what I saw today. Exactly what my mother is like. I don't want to. But I think I have to."

Silence.

"How does my father go there every day? How can he sit there? I could barely stand it."

Silence.

"And the worst thing is," I whispered, "I don't think I can go back."

"You don't have to."

"Really?"

"Yes. You don't have to."

"But my father goes every day. Every day." I burst into tears again. "And I should. I should want to spend the time with her."

Silence.

"But, Gail, it's not her. That's what is so awful. It's not her at all. It's just whiteness, vacant, empty whiteness."

Silence.

"Tell me," Gail said.

I told her. And we both cried. And we went downstairs to the kitchen to eat ice cream.

"At home we have it with whipped cream and nuts," I said.

Gail laughed and let me have the whole pint of coffee. She ate the vanilla.

Andrew ran into the kitchen.

"Mindy, Mindy, you never came to see my homework!"

"Sorry, Andrew. Can I see it now?"

"Here it is!" He waved a paper under my nose. "I wrote an essay about my favorite animal. Gail didn't help me at all."

"I'd love to see it."

"*The Three Told Sloth*, by Andrew Burke," I read.

"It's three-toed sloth," I said.

"That's what I wrote."

"No, you wrote 'three told.'"

"What are you saying?"

"Toed, three toes. This sloth has only three toes."

"Really? Only three toes? I thought it meant he had three stories told about him. You know, like twice told tales—but better."

"Nope. Toes. Three toes. How come he's your favorite animal?"

"Read and you'll see. Sloths are cool." Andrew sat down next to me. "Go ahead," he said. "Read."

*The three told sloth is one of my very favorite mammals. I think mammals may be my very favorite kind of animal of all. Mammals have fur and live babies. Live babies are the best kind.*

Live mothers, too, I thought. Stop it, stop it and read.

*The three told sloth lives in the jungle. Mostly they hang upside down in trees. Here's the main thing about them. They move very very slow. That's why if you are being lazy or slow someone might call YOU a sloth. But when you finish reading this, you will know that if someone does call you a sloth, it's OK. Sloths are not bad. They're just very very slow. In fact, most of the time they don't move at all, they just hang upside down from a tree. Sometimes they hang there for so long that mossy stuff grows right on them, right on their fur, like they were a rock.*

*Sloths only eat herbs. They are herbivorous. That means they don't eat meat, so they don't kill other animals. That's good, because they are very very slow, if you remember what I just told you.*

*So mostly sloths hang around in the trees. They sleep during the day, but they don't do very much at night either. They have to stop just hanging from a tree when they have to go to the bathroom, both numbers one and two. They can't do that hanging upside down! But they only have to do that once a week!*

*So all in all, sloths are my favorite mammals, for all the reasons I already wrote.*

*The End*

"So? Isn't it good? See, I did the introduction, that's the first paragraph. Then the body. Then the conclusion, that's the last paragraph."

"You did great," I said, and gave him a big hug. "Just great. I'm very proud of you."

It was my mother's voice coming out of my mouth. "I'm very proud of you." I would never hear her say that again.

Gail lent me her favorite nightgown, long and white, with tiny pink rosebuds at the neck. I called my father's friend Harry to tell him where I was, in case my father called and couldn't find me. I knew he talked to Harry every day. I doubted he would call me, but if he did, he would be really mad if he couldn't find me. Harry said he would tell him.

Gail and I got into her twin beds, and her mother came in and kissed us both good-night. "Sleep tight. Don't let the bedbugs bite," I heard my mother say.

When I woke up the next morning, Gail was sketching again. I watched her.

"I wish I had something I loved as much as you love drawing," I whispered.

Silence.

I closed my eyes. I saw my mother in her hospital room. I opened my eyes.

"I better go home," I said. "I should check the mail from yesterday."

"Wanna go to the movies later? I have to go to church at noon, but we could go later," Gail said, without looking up from her drawing.

"Sure. What's playing?"

"*Splendor in the Grass,* I think."

"Neat."

"I'll call and get the times. Call you later."

"Okay."

I put on my clothes from yesterday and walked out the front door. My mother's car was parked in front. Why was my mother here? She never came to Gail's house. Then I remembered it was me driving her car. I had left it there yesterday. I got in and drove home.

There was a lot of mail. I sorted through it. My college applications had begun to arrive. I piled them all up on the window seat. My pile was as big as my mother's today. What should I do with her pile? Should I put it with my father's? Should I keep it separate? I sat on the window seat, staring at the three piles. Three of us. There were three of us. There were always three of us. There had to be three piles. I left them there and walked into the living room. The candy dish was still empty, but everything else was the same, as if my mother were still here in the house, fluffing up seat cushions and emptying ashtrays. I went upstairs to her room, to their room. Everything there was the same, too. My mother's jewelry box was still on her dresser; Uncle Irving's picture was still on her desk; the sachet I had made in second grade was still in the back of her underwear drawer; her big bottle of Jean Naté was still in their bathroom. I went to my room and lay down on my bed. It all seemed wrong. Her things should have been with her or at least look different now. But they didn't. They were all exactly as they always were.

The phone rang.
"It's *Spartacus*," Gail said.

"What's *Spartacus*?"

"What's playing. Not *Splendor in the Grass*. Want to go anyway?"

*Spartacus*. After I had refused in Cape Cod. After I had not gone to the last movie I could have gone to with my mother.

"Honey, look, *Spartacus* is playing. It's right down the road, and it starts in a half hour," my father had announced.

"Perfect," my mother had said, rubbing her neck. "I've been dying to see it."

"I haven't been dying to see it," I had said. "I don't want to see it. I hate blood-and-guts movies."

"It's about freedom, Mindy. About a slave's fight for freedom against oppression."

"I don't care. It's all going to be blood-and-guts, anyway. Boring. I'd rather stay in the motel and read."

"Mindy?" Gail said.

"Yeah, I guess," I said.

"Good. Meet you there at three. I have to run errands first."

She hung up.

*Spartacus*.

❧

I got to the theater early. I walked. It would probably be dark by the time we got out and I wouldn't be able to drive home. I waited outside, looking at the movie posters.

White. Everything in her room is white. Bright white. Too bright. Blinding white.

A tap on my shoulder, and I jumped.

"I always seem to scare you," Bobby said. "Sorry."

"I'm just jumpy." I smiled. "Sorry."

Silence.

"You going to see the movie?" I asked.

Bobby smiled.

"Right. Why else would you be here, in front of the movie theater?"

"Right," he said. "Are you waiting for someone?"

"Yeah, Gail."

Silence.

"We thought *Splendor in the Grass* was playing, but it turns out to be *Spartacus.*"

God, I sounded so stupid.

White.

"Didn't you want to see *Spartacus?*" he asked.

"No. Not exactly. Not my kind of movie," I said.

Not now. Not when I should have seen it in Cape Cod.

"This is my fourth time," he said. "I love this movie."

"Why?" I asked. "I mean, what about it do you like so much?"

"Everything. First of all, I love Howard Fast. He's been my hero for years. He wrote *The Passion of Sacco and Vanzetti*. And he wrote the book the movie is based on. He was blacklisted, but he never named names. He went to jail for three years instead."

White.

"God, you know a lot," I blurted out. "Sorry. I'm impressed. I mean, really. Me, I think reading *Peyton Place* is a big political statement."

Shut up, Mindy. Just shut up.

Bobby laughed.

I prayed for Gail to arrive and save me from my idiocy. And from the white room.

"My father taught me all about the McCarthy hearings, told me who were the good guys and who were the bad guys. He was a writer back then."

Silence.

Just talk. Ask questions. Stop thinking about the white room.

"What does he do now?" I asked.

"He still writes a little, but he hasn't been able to earn a living doing it for years. We moved up here so he could go to work for my uncle and my mother could stop working."

"Oh."

Go on. Keep talking.

"What does your uncle do?"

"He runs a furniture store in North Roseville."

"Oh."

White.

Where is Gail?

Bobby looked at his watch. "Shouldn't we get tickets? The show starts in five minutes."

"I don't know what to do about Gail," I said, looking up and down Tamarack Street.

"Maybe she'll just be late. She could find us inside."

"I guess."

But where was she?

White.

Bobby went up to the box office and bought his ticket. I started to follow him, and I saw Gail running toward us.

"Sorry, sorry. I was drawing and I lost all track of time. Ran all the way. Here I am. Sorry." She looked at Bobby. "Hi."

"Hi," he said.

We stopped at the candy counter. Gail and I each got popcorn and Bobby bought a Sky Bar. The previews were on as we walked into the theater.

"No second feature today. *Spartacus* is too long," Bobby whispered.

My mother sat through the whole three hours with her neck in pain.

We found seats in the fifth row and settled in, Gail, me, and Bobby.

# Chapter Six

THE CURTAINS CLOSED AND stayed closed. Music came on.

Watch the movie. Just think about the movie.

"The overture," Bobby whispered.

"It's a movie," I said. "Movies don't have overtures."

"This one does," he said.

Gail poked me.

"Overture," I whispered.

"Very classical for an overture," she whispered. "Not very bouncy," she added, and leaned back in her seat.

Finally, the music stopped. The curtain opened, and the credits started.

"See?" Bobby poked me. "Dalton Trumbo. The screenwriter. He was one of the Hollywood Ten. And see?" Another poke. "Based on the novel by Howard Fast."

Did my mother know all this?

Gail poked me. "What?"

My arms were going to be black and blue.

"The screenwriter was one of the Hollywood Ten."

"The Hollywood Ten what?"

"Shh. I don't know. We'll ask Bobby later."

Sand for as far as you could see. People working in the heat of the sun, sweating, fainting.

". . . the disease called human slavery." Bobby poked me. "See. It's about slavery. It's not just blood and guts. It's about freedom."

"You know what Robert Frost said about freedom?" my father had asked.

My mother had been awake, but she had looked groggy. She was in traction, in the hospital, the first hospital.

"They let me out of my harness for a while," she told me.

I saw some leather straps hanging off the bed.

"It looks like some medieval torture thing," I said.

"Straight out of *Spartacus*." My father laughed.

My mother laughed and closed her eyes. "Roman, not medieval," she whispered.

"He said that freedom is feeling at ease in one's harness."

I poked Bobby. "Where is Thrace?"

"Where Greece and Turkey are now," he said. He knew everything.

Gail poked me. "I wanted to know where Thrace was and Bobby told me," I whispered.

"Just past thrice," Gail whispered.

"Greece," I said.

"Shh," Bobby whispered. "Watch this. It's great."

"I am not an animal," Kirk Douglas said, as his owners were treating him like one. "I am not an animal."

"All we want is to get out of this damn country," he said.

People in the desert. Lots of people. Lots of desert. The screen flashed "Intermission." The lights came on.

"See," said Bobby. "Isn't it great?"

"Yes, it is," I said.

"It is pretty bloody," Gail objected. "Why did Laurence Olivier have to slash that slave's neck? Yech."

"To show how brutish slaveholding is, how inhuman, how savage."

"Well, it worked," Gail said. "Let's get something to drink. All that desert makes me thirsty."

We got up, went to the snack bar, got Cokes, and came back to our seats.

"Do you like it?" Bobby asked me.

"More than I thought I would," I said. Much more. "I loved what he said about all people dying, that everyone loses when they die, but that for slaves, their only freedom is death. The guy is a good screenwriter."

"He is not an animal," said Bobby, and we all laughed.

"So what is the Hollywood Ten?" Gail asked.

"A bunch of screenwriters blacklisted in the forties by HUAC."

"HUAC?"

"The House Un-American Activities Committee."

"Who are *they*?"

The lights dimmed. "Tell you later," Bobby whispered. We leaned back to watch.

The slaves, the ex-slaves, fought and fought, and played and walked, and buried their dead, and then they had to fight some more, but there were so many of them now. And then they were beaten. So many dead, I could hardly look at the screen. Everything was lost. And then: "I am Spartacus. I am Spartacus. I am Spartacus. I am Spartacus." I burst into tears. Bobby patted my hand.

"Isn't it great?" he asked.

I nodded and turned to Gail. Tears were streaming down her cheeks. I touched her hand.

"When just one man says 'No, I won't,' Rome begins to fear. We were tens of thousands who said 'No.' That was the wonder of it," said Kirk Douglas.

"And now they're dead," said Tony Curtis.

Bobby poked me. "Great lines," he said. "Dalton Trumbo."

I couldn't stop crying. Had my mother cried that night?

∾

When the credits were over, the music stopped, the lights came on again. We still sat there in our seats, exhausted. Bobby beamed at us.

"See what I mean? Powerful, huh?"

"Powerful, yeah. I can hardly move," I said. I felt like a strand of overcooked spaghetti, limp and drained. Had my mother felt that way?

"Let's go get a soda or something," Bobby said.

"How can you be so cheery?" Gail asked. "I just want to keep crying."

"I've seen it four times now. It gets better, and it takes less of a toll. Let's go."

We made our way out of the theater. It was dusk, clear but dim. Chilly.

"Let's go someplace close, real close," Gail said. "I'm freezing."

"Smitty's," I said, pointing across the street.

We got a booth and huddled inside our jackets until we warmed up a bit.

"So, are you a big movie expert?" Gail asked Bobby as we looked at the menus. "I don't know why I always look at the menu when I know exactly what I want."

"Don't mind her," I told Bobby. "She really does want you to answer the question. She just doesn't like to stop talking until she has to."

Gail stuck her tongue out at me.

Bobby laughed. "Who does?" he asked.

Me, I thought. I'd much rather keep my mouth shut. My mother would, too.

We ordered french fries and cherry Cokes.

"I don't know if you could call me an expert," Bobby began. "But I do love movies. Movies, books, and rock 'n' roll."

"Neat," Gail said.

Our Cokes arrived. Bobby blew the wrapper on his straw at my nose.

"Missed," I said, and blew mine back. I wasn't looking, and Gail got me right in the ear.

"Neat-o," Bobby said.

Gail bowed her head.

"Ring the bell," I said.

"I never heard that one," Bobby said.

"My old boyfriend," Gail said. "Anytime anyone said, 'Neat-o,' he said, 'Ring the bell.' It was like a reflex with him. Now Mindy says it all the time, too."

"Pavlov and his dogs," I said. "Woof."

We laughed and slurped our Cokes.

"So what is this Un-American thing you were whispering about?" Gail asked.

"The House Un-American Activities Committee, HUAC. They started investigating communism in Hollywood in 1947. The Hollywood Ten were screenwriters, most of them really good, who HUAC ordered to testify about their lives and to name names."

"Name what names?" I asked.

"Name the names of people they knew, their friends, who would then be investigated for being Communists."

"Were they Communists?"

"Some had been, back in the thirties, during the Depression, when a lot of people were. But HUAC was interested in smearing people, and the Hollywood Ten refused to testify. They were all sent to jail for contempt."

"Oh, wow," I said. "McCarthyism even before McCarthy."

"Yep," Bobby said.

I knew about McCarthy. My mother had insisted that my father buy our first TV so that she could watch the Army-McCarthy hearings. She watched them every day. And she had a record called *The Investigator*. It had only a title, no credits, nothing written on the back at all. It was all talking, a guy doing a good imitation of Joe McCarthy who dies in an airplane crash, goes to heaven, and starts investigating God.

Stop thinking about her. Stop it.

"What was it like, living in the big city?" Gail asked.

"It was fun," Bobby said. "Lots of things to do, lots of noise, lots of kids."

"Do you miss it?"

"Yeah, at first it was real hard. We moved here in August, and I didn't meet any kids until school started. That was bad. I went to the library every day and to every movie that came along. You don't get as many movies here."

"We know," Gail and I said together.

"And you have no good rock 'n' roll stations. I used to listen to Murray the K and his Swingin' Soiree every day. I miss that a lot. And my friends."

Did he have a girlfriend back in New York who he missed desperately? Some beautiful tall blond brilliant cheerleader who got straight *A*s and read the *New York Times* every day?

"Do you have a girlfriend?" Gail asked, making loud slurping noises.

Our french fries arrived. I made a big puddle of

ketchup in the corner of my plate and waited for the fries to cool down. Bobby sprayed ketchup all over his. Gail salted hers. No ketchup.

"Yeah, sort of," Bobby answered. "But we broke up when I moved."

Silence.

"Take good care of my baby," Gail sang.

"We weren't doing so well, anyway," Bobby said with a shrug. "But I had this bunch of guys I hung out with who I really miss. I played on my high school basketball team."

"Have you tried out here yet?" I asked.

"I talked to Coach D'Amato Friday. Tryouts start next week."

"Good luck," Gail and I said together.

"Thanks," said Bobby.

The fries were the perfect temperature, and we gobbled them down. This was nice, comfortable, warm. Like an Archie and Veronica comic book. Friends hanging out at Ye Olde Soda Shoppe. Except none of their mothers was in a white room, staring at a wall and leaking tears.

The waitress brought the check. We split it three ways and bundled up again.

"Where do you live?" I asked Bobby as we were going out the door.

"North Roseville," he said. "See you tomorrow," and he turned left on Spruce Street. Gail and I ran to the bus stop on the next block.

"He's so nice," she said.

"Yeah. And he knows so much."

Silence.

"Isn't it amazing how little we know about stuff?" she asked.

"And how much he does," I said. "Makes you want to move to New York."

"I don't think you just absorb it by living there," Gail said. "I think he'd know stuff no matter where he lived."

The bus came before we froze, and we rode home in silence.

❧

My father called from Syracuse soon after I got home.

"I'm going to start on my college applications tonight," I told him.

"Good. Excellent."

Silence.

"I called to see if you had thought any more about seeing your mother," he said.

Yes. I thought a lot about it.

"Yes. I drove up to see her yesterday morning," I said.

"You did? By yourself? The nurses didn't tell me." He sounded annoyed about that.

"Well, I did."

"Was it early in the morning? I must have been at the office," he said. "Well, that's good. Good. I'm sure she appreciated it."

How would she know?

"It was very hard," I said. Don't say anything else. That's all he wants to hear.

"Yes. I understand. But I'm glad you saw her."

I don't know if I am.

"I'll be home tomorrow night. We'll go out to dinner together. We need to think about what to do after. Okay?"

He meant after she died.

"Okay."

"Take care, Neenie. Bye."

Bye.

# CHAPTER SEVEN

THE COLLEGE APPLICATIONS WERE stacked up on the window seat. Better than thinking about the white room. I took them upstairs.

So many questions. So much they wanted to know. *Your Mother: Is she living?* How was I supposed to answer that? Yes, I wrote "Yes" in big letters. Yes, she is living, yes, she is alive, but she is not herself. She is not alive as herself. She is alive without being herself at all. Yes, just write "Yes."

*YOUR SPACE. Please use this side of the form in your own way.*

EAT SHIT. I wrote "EAT SHIT" in big, dark letters. I stared at the words. When I was five, I had been furious at my mother, I don't remember why. I had written her a note and slipped it under her door. The note said, "SHIT TO YOU, MOTHER. SHIT SHIT SHIT TO YOU." I didn't know what *shit* meant, but I knew it was a bad word. Even writing it was bad. I never said it out loud. But I knew writing it would get to her. My mother never mentioned it then. But years later I found the note in her desk. She had saved it, along with some clay ashtrays and recipe covers I had made in kindergarten.

I looked at the next application.

*Comments that only family members can make.* "Your mother or father" was supposed to write this part. I would have to write it. My father would refuse. I would write it and ask him to read it, correct it, help me with it. Maybe he would. Maybe he would help me with this.

*I love my daughter, Mindy, very much.* [He would have to call me Mindy in the application essay.] *She is a wonderful, bright, perky girl, and of course I recommend her highly as an applicant. Mindy's mother is dying of a brain tumor now, which has not been easy for Mindy, but she has met even this challenge with her usual straightforwardness and determination. She will be fine.* [This sounded like my father. Fine, she will be fine.]

*When Mindy was in nursery school, her teacher told us the following story, which I feel is indicative of who my daughter is and why you should accept her application. The kids in the class were squabbling over the toy instruments in the room. The teacher kept trying to organize the play but failed, as at least a few of the children kept demanding to be the leader of the band they were trying to start. Finally, Mindy put her arms up and said, "Okay. Let's make a band, and you (pointing to one of the children who had not been disruptive) be the leader." That was it. All the kids took their instruments and fell into line. "The best kind of leader," said her teacher, "is one who organizes others, not one who aggrandizes herself. You have a wonderful child." Her mother and I were very proud of her then, and we still are.* [He would include my mother, even now, would speak for her when she couldn't.] *She* is *a great kid.*

That was practically word for word the way he always told that story about me.

"It's what's in here," he would say, patting his heart, "that really counts." He would say this as he opened my report card and made a big fuss about not looking at my grades first. He would turn to the back page of my report card, where you got checked off as good or bad in "relates to others," "is considerate." The social skills. Of course I always got checked "Good." Everyone did. But my father acted like it was such a big deal. And my straight *A*s never counted as much—until my sophomore year in high school, when I got a *C* in social studies. Then, all of a sudden, grades were crucial. I had to get good grades to get into a good college.

Before I was born, I was supposed to be a boy. They

were so sure I was a boy that they had only picked a boy's name—Irving, after my mother's brother. My father was disappointed when I turned out to be a girl, so he pretended I wasn't. He taught me to ride a boy's bike, bought me boy's swimming trunks, took me to a barber until I was eleven, taught me to throw like a boy and drive a stick shift. He was the best dad. I was not going to grow up to be waifish and weak, like my mother. No, I would grow up to be tough and independent, like my dad. I did sit-ups and push-ups with him, shot hoops in the driveway. We went fishing together, just us guys. My mother would pack us a lunch. But puberty put an end to this camaraderie. Once I grew breasts, he dumped me.

My mother had leaned back against her hospital pillows, in the first hospital, when they thought she had a sprained neck or, at worst, spinal meningitis.

"How was school? Your first day as a senior. You have grown up so fast, sweetie. It seems like yesterday when I first walked you to kindergarten." Her eyes had filled. She stared at me, but she was seeing something else, something far away, something only she could see. She was alone there, wherever she was. Even before we knew the worst.

"Gail and I got Miss Dwyer for English. And we

got lunch together and Miss O'Lanan for Latin. We're reading Virgil."

"*Arma virumque cano*," my mother said. " 'Of arms and the man I sing.' The *Aeneid*."

How did she know that?

"And Miss O'Lanan said she would read *Winne ille Pu* with us," I said.

"Oh, sweetie, remember when I used to read you the Pooh books? And you loved sad old Eeyore and always petted the picture of him to cheer him up? You were always such a sweet girl. So considerate."

I hated being called considerate. It was my mother's favorite thing to be. It always made me feel like a jerk, like a cross between Goody Two-Shoes and Florence Nightingale. I loved Eeyore and felt sorry for him, that's all. I wasn't being good, I wasn't saving people. I just liked the sad old donkey.

My mother kept staring at me. I had run out of school things to tell her. We sat silently.

"That sweater looks so pretty on you, sweetie. You have always looked beautiful in pink. Even as a baby."

"Yeah, I got a lot of compliments on this sweater today. I should wear it more often."

My mother sat forward. "Who?" she asked. "Who gave you compliments?"

"Who?"

"Yes. Who said you looked good?"

"I don't remember. Lots of kids."

"Who?" my mother demanded to know.

"Well, Yuri did."

"Who's Yuri?"

Why was it so important that I tell her if she didn't even know who I was talking about?

"He's an exchange student from Russia."

"A boy?"

"Yeah."

"And the others?" she demanded. "Were they all boys?"

I couldn't remember. Mostly it had just been a feeling, a kind of nice glow that hung over me during the day, a glow that made me feel pretty. But who had actually said I looked pretty? I couldn't remember.

"I think so, but I don't really remember. Why?"

"Because, sweetie, when boys tell you you look pretty, believe them." My mother leaned back again. "But when girls tell you you look pretty in something, never wear it again. Girls want you to look bad. They are competing for the boys. If a boy says you look pretty, listen to him." My mother closed her eyes.

She had never said anything like that before. She'd always encouraged me to have girlfriends, to talk to them. Is this how she felt about her women friends? Did she think Gert from next door was trying to steal my father?

Her eyes were still closed. I picked up the paper that was sitting on the other visitor's chair. I turned the pages very quietly so as not to disturb her.

"Look at the obituaries," she said, her eyes still closed. "Gary Cooper died. I was in tears the whole morning. I loved that man. What an actor. So versatile, so handsome, so strong. I can't believe he died. When I was a girl, he was my favorite. We went ape about him, as you would say."

Why couldn't grown-ups use teenage words correctly? Why did they always sound so foreign in a grown-up's mouth?

"Not ape about, Mom. No one goes ape about anyone. You just go ape."

"Well, *we* went ape *about* Gary Cooper. What a man. Your uncle Irving looked just like him."

Even though my uncle Irving had died at age twenty-one, before I was born, I knew more about him than I did about most of my living relatives. My mother told me story after story. He was tall (six feet), thin, and a little clumsy. He loved gardenias. He cracked his first joke at the age of three: "If a nanny goat had no nose, how would it smell?" The answer:

"Terrrrrrrrible." When my cousin Robert was born and everyone said how much he looked like his father, Irving went to the hospital and announced that he looked nothing like his father—too much hair and no glasses. My mother had adored him.

"Look at the picture of him," she said. "Just like Irving. So handsome."

I turned to the obituaries. My grandfather used to say he read the obituaries first thing in the morning to see if he was dead. Then he got up and brushed his teeth.

"There's nothing about Gary Cooper, Mom," I said. "I think Gary Cooper died in the spring." I had some vague memory of that—some famous actor like that. John Wayne? No, he was still alive. But my mother had just read the paper this morning. What was wrong with her?

My mother's eyes flew open. "You're right. This medicine is making me crazy. He did die in the spring. Just like Irving. May. Early May. I guess I was just thinking about Irving. Irving loved Chico Marx. He was his favorite of the Marx brothers. He used to imitate the way he played the piano, the way he would shoot the keys with his index finger. Harpo was my favorite. Not the harp so much, but that funny look on his face, or when he pulled enormous things out of his pants pockets." She sighed. "And Irving and I always thought our mother looked like Margaret Dumont."

I laughed. "She does," I said. Tall, proud, so proper, so cold, her nose held so high that she looks down at everything and everyone.

"Cold and stupid," she whispered. "So cold. I hate her. She's like those Steiff stuffed animals she used to send you. They cost a lot, and they look sweet, but they're hard. You can't cuddle with them. And you are supposed to cuddle with them. They are stuffed animals, for God's sake. But they are hard. Hard as nails." She was almost talking to herself. "She never cried when Irving died. Not one tear. I never forgave her for that. And I never will." My mother closed her eyes again.

I stared at her. There was so much I didn't know about this woman. This is my mother. I thought I knew everything there was to know about her: her favorite color (navy blue), that she drank her tea with no sugar, that she practically bathed in Jean Naté, that she wore a padded bra, that she hated to cook, that she thought of herself as homely, that she set out my father's clothes for the next day, that she was an okay bridge player and a terrible golfer. But I never knew she hated her mother. No one liked my grandmother. There was nothing likable about her. She was all stiff and proper and hard. But my mother wrote her a letter every single day. What did she say in them?

"Remember when we used to visit Irving's grave," she said, opening her eyes. "Just you and me. We brought gardenias and we would sit on his headstone and I would tell you all about him, all about your wonderful uncle whom you never knew. The uncle you would have loved so much."

"Yes, I remember." I used to love those stories.

"He would have thought you were the cat's pajamas." She paused and closed her eyes. "He would have gone ape about you." She started to snore very softly. She had looked so pale against the stark white hospital sheets.

*If you could invite any well-known person, past or present, to dinner, who would it be and why?*

My mother. I can't think of anyone else but my mother. So many questions I would ask her. I can't write this down, I can't pretend that my mother is/was a well-known person. But she is the one person, past or present, I would want to invite to dinner.

Why? Because I can't, because I can never, ever invite her to dinner to discuss anything. And because while I could, I didn't want to. I didn't think she had anything to say that I wanted to hear. Now I have so many questions.

Did she love me even when we were fighting about everything? Did she think I was the biggest brat she ever met? Was she glad she didn't have more kids because they would all turn out to be like me? Did she hate me for wanting her to be Donna Reed, give me a brother like Andrew and a warm father? Was she happy with her life? Did she want anything else? Did she know how hard I tried not to be like her, to never wear perfume, to not have "sayings," to never wince? Did she know how determined I was to grow up and be different, to not be a housewife who listened to her husband tell every detail of his day at dinner every night?

What was she sorry about, what would she have changed if she could have lived long enough? Why didn't she buy me that dress I had wanted when I was six—the blue taffeta with the white puffy sleeves? Did she think the fighting was all my fault? What did she want me to be? What did she think I *would* be? Was she mad that I hadn't gone to see her again? Did she know that I was there when I did? Was she happy to see my father when he came home every night? Did she love him? What college did she think I should go to? What did she think I should major in? What colors did she think I looked best in? Why did we fight so much?

What would she have written about me in *"Comments that only family members can make"*? What was her favorite memory of me? Did she remember when I was little and we squeezed hands?

∾

*Monday*
*November 20, 1961*

The next night my father and I sat across a table from each other at Frimaldi's. I had the essay in my pocketbook, the college essay I had written for him.

We used to come here when I was little. I would stuff myself on the homemade bread and not even touch the spaghetti and meatballs when they finally came. But now it was different. My mother wasn't here. It was just me and him, me and the man who had excused himself from my adolescence. We were both silent.

I heard my mother's voice ask, "What's the scuttlebutt at the Imperial?" That's how a meal was supposed to begin. That's what I was supposed to say now. I stuffed a piece of hot, soft bread into my mouth. My father pushed the butter plate toward me. I pushed it back.

"So, how have you been?" he asked.

How have I been?

"I've been trying to write my college applications."
I began slowly. I opened my pocketbook and fingered
the essay.

"Good. Good."

My father shook a cigarette from his pack. He
tapped it on the table. Once, twice, three times. He always tapped three times.

I waited.

He took the matches from the ashtray on the table.
He lit the match, lit the cigarette, took a long drag,
watched the match burn down to his fingertips, then
blew it out. He always lit a cigarette the same way. It
took forever. He had a procedure for everything. When
he peed, he flushed the toilet in the middle of his pee-
ing. He had it timed perfectly, so that his pee stream
ended just as the water came into the bowl. I always
wondered how he could time it so perfectly.

He took another drag.

"Do you want to know where I'm applying?"

"Of course I do, Neenie. You sound so angry."

His voice had that oily, slimy sound I hated so
much. Scary. It was his scary tone.

Angry? Me? No, it's just that my mother is dying
and I am applying to college all alone and you have deserted me as much as she has.

"No. I'm not angry."

"So, tell me about the applications. How are they coming?"

I knew he didn't care. I knew I meant less to him than a speck of dirt.

"I'm doing them," I said. "It's hard."

"But you're doing them. That's good."

Good. I was doing them. That was all that mattered. They would get done, I would get in somewhere, and everything would continue to look normal. But this was abnormal. My life had turned abnormal with the abnormal thing in my mother's brain.

"And how is school going?"

"No," I said. "I'm not finished talking about the college applications."

He stared at me. I had never talked to him like this. And now I couldn't stop.

"You don't even know where I'm applying. Don't you want to know?"

He kept staring at me. I stared back.

"Neenie, what is wrong?" More oiliness. How could a voice be so oily?

"What is wrong? Everything. Everything is wrong."

He kept staring me down, willing me to lower my voice with his eyes. We were in public. It was bad enough to make a scene in private, but here we were in public.

"Dad, I need help with this. I don't even know if I have the right applications. I don't know where I want to go to college. Please."

"Didn't you talk to your adviser at school?"

"Yes, but I still don't know what I want. Mom and I had talked about it a little, but we never settled on which schools."

My mother had been pushing small colleges. I had wanted to apply only to schools in New York City. Now I didn't know. Had I just been being obstinate, picking the opposite of what she wanted?

He leaned back in his chair, inhaled.

"Whatever you want is fine," he said. "You know I trust you. You have a good head on your shoulders. You'll be fine." He smiled and took another drag.

"But I want some help," I said.

"Call Uncle Steve. He works at Arcadia Junior College and knows a lot. He'll help you."

I stared at him.

"I'll call him if you want," he said.

I snapped my pocketbook shut.

Vinny, our waiter, came over, and we ordered. I took another piece of the warm, soft bread.

"Butter it, Neenie. It's so much better that way."

"I like it plain," I said, and stuffed another piece into my mouth.

"No, you don't," he said. "You always put tons of butter on it. When you were little, you ate it with so much butter we had to wash your hands before you could hold a spoon." He laughed.

"Now I like it this way," I said. And crammed another piece in.

My father buttered his piece slowly, so that the butter completely covered it. There was no white showing. He took a bite and put the bread back down on his plate.

"I'm different, Dad," I said.

"Different? What do you mean?"

"I'm different from when I was little."

"Well. Of course you are, Neenie. Of course."

"Yes, of course." My voice was getting louder. My father looked hard at me. I knew I should shut up, but I couldn't.

"I mean Mom's being sick is very hard, Dad. I'm only sixteen. I feel lost."

"Well, of course you do, honey. Of course. But you'll be okay. You're a *shtarker*, like your dad."

Once when I was little and had just learned to swim, my father had been watching a bunch of us playing in a shallow lake. There was one wild boy who kept trying to drown us one after the other. He was really strong, and he held me under for a long time. I fought him with all my strength. I finally got loose and looked up for my father. He was sitting on the dock laughing at me. The boy attacked my friend Judy next, and my father jumped right in to save her.

"Why didn't you save *me*?" I had asked him.

"Because you are strong. I don't worry about you. You can take care of yourself."

"But I was scared!" I cried.

"But you're okay. You took care of yourself. You're fine." He had laughed some more.

He sat there now, smiling at me. But it wasn't at me, not the me I lived with. It was Neenie, the little girl who waited for her daddy to come home each night, who ran through the house when she heard his car drive up, yelling, "My daddy, my daddy, my daddy!" The little thing who would jump into his arms and cling to him like a monkey, until he unhooked me and plunked me down so he could kiss my mother. And cling to her.

"Why did Mom have a nervous breakdown?" I asked.

"What? What nervous breakdown?"

"You know, when I was five, she had a nervous breakdown. What does that mean?"

"Where did you hear that?" He smiled. "She never had a nervous breakdown."

"Yes, she did. When I had that baby-sitter who put my hair in braids. Mom always referred to it. You know, 'when we remodeled the house and I had a nervous breakdown.' I just never knew what it meant."

His mouth got smaller, and he tried to make it smile.

"Neenie, that was nothing. She never had a nervous breakdown."

"Then why did she call it that?" My voice was getting higher again.

"It was nothing. She was just exhausted from working so hard on decorating the house. That's all. Nothing more than that." He leaned back in his chair. The conversation was over.

Well, not my end of it.

"Why did she see Dr. Wolf?"

He sat up straight and began buttering another piece of bread. I waited.

"All the women in town saw Dr. Wolf," he said quietly. "It was just something that they all did."

"But why did Mom? Did she start seeing him when she had her nervous breakdown?" I couldn't let it go. I had heard the term *nervous breakdown* as a child. One of those big words that make no sense. Like when I thought the Tappan Zee bridge we drove over to get to Westchester was an animal named the Tappan Zebra.

"I told you, she didn't have a nervous breakdown," he said, staring at me.

But it did him no good. I knew. I had always known. I knew because I knew how long I had known that word. Nervous breakdown. I had known that word forever. I had known it before it meant anything at all. I had known it the way I knew the words to *Guys and Dolls,* insisting that they were singing Nation Detroit, not Nathan Detroit. Nathan Detroit made no sense. It had to be Nation. Nation was a country, Detroit was a city. They went together. And so did my mother and her nervous breakdown. They had been there, together, in my childhood. No matter how much he denied it, I knew. I knew.

❧

Vinny brought my spaghetti and meatballs and my father's broiled scrod.

"*Bon appétit,*" he said.

"It looks wonderful," my father said to Vinnie. "Just wonderful." He smiled that warm smile he used with strangers. Vinny smiled back and left us.

I was full. I had stuffed myself on the bread. The enormous bowl of pasta and meat looked overwhelming.

My father crushed his cigarette in the ashtray and started in on his fish.

I readjusted my napkin and took the fork in my right hand, the soup spoon in my left, the way my mother had taught me to twirl the really long pasta they always served at Frimaldi's. I twirled one spoonful on my fork. Perfect. I scraped the twirl back into the bowl. I didn't think I could eat a bite.

"How's your spaghetti?" my father asked.

"Good. It's fine. Like always," I said. I traded my spoon for a knife and started to cut up the meatballs.

"Did I ever tell you about my high school football team?" my father asked.

I nodded.

"We were the only football team that had Jewish players, Neenie. That was our advantage. We could call the plays in Yiddish."

I heard my mother's voice ask, "But how did the non-Jewish boys on your team understand?"

I stuffed more bread in my mouth.

"The non-Jewish boys on the team had to learn Yiddish," my father announced proudly. "What accents! *Aintz, tzvei, drei, feir, varf der knaidel* out of here. The goyim made *knaidel* sound like a fancy mixed drink."

Just listen, I thought. That's all you have to do.

"You don't have to like it, you just have to eat it," I heard my mother say.

"I ran seventy yards for a touchdown to win the game against Albany. Only goyim played for Albany. They didn't understand a word we said."

You don't have to like it, I thought. You just have to sit here.

# CHAPTER EIGHT

*Monday*
*December 11, 1961*

"WHERE DO YOU GO every day after school?" Bobby asked me in the school cafeteria.

"I drive around," I said, glancing at Gail.

"Where?"

"Just around. Anywhere."

"Can I come sometime?"

Could he? I wasn't sure. I had never thought of asking anyone to come with me.

"It's okay if you don't want me to," he said, ducking his head shyly, trying not to look embarrassed. "Sorry I asked."

"No, it's okay. Sure, come. I play the radio real loud, though."

"Fine with me," he said, grinning.

Was it fine with me? I wondered. Or did I just not want to make him feel bad? I wasn't sure. I decided it didn't matter.

I waited for Bobby in the car. He got in and turned the radio up. "There'd be days like this, Mama said," he sang along.

Maybe this would be fun.

"We'll drive to the Hinkley Reservoir," I told him as I put the car in gear. "It's about as far as we can go and still get back before dark."

"Neat-o," he said.

"Ring the bell," I answered.

"Woof, woof," we said together and laughed.

"Pretty country," Bobby said.

"Yeah."

"Who put the bomp in the bomp shoo bomp . . ."

"Basketball practice starts next week," Bobby said. "I made the team."

"Great."

Maybe my father was right. Maybe I should have been a boy. Then I could be playing basketball and baseball and running around, not feeling like I was slogging through pea soup.

"Are you okay?" Bobby asked.

"What do you mean?"

"I mean, usually you're more talkative."

"No, I'm not. That's Gail."

"I can tell the difference," said Bobby.

"Sorry. I didn't mean to jump you."

"Is it your mom? Gail told me she was sick. How is she doing?"

Damn Gail. I didn't want to talk about it, especially to someone who didn't know anything. How is she doing? She's doing terrible. She's dying, for God's sake.

"What did she tell you?" I snapped.

"I'm sorry. We don't have to talk about this."

"What did she tell you?" The bigmouth.

"Hardly anything. Just that your mother was in the hospital. That's it."

Damn her. If she was going to blab, she could have at least told him the whole story.

"She has a brain tumor. She's dying," I blurted out.

"Oh, my God, I'm so sorry. I didn't know. I thought she was just a little sick. Oh, Mindy, I'm so sorry." He patted me on the shoulder. "No wonder you got so mad when I asked you."

"I didn't get mad," I said. Yes, I did.

"Do you want to talk about something else?" he asked. "Or do you want to talk about your mother?"

Both. The tears started to well up behind my eyes. My fingers clutched the steering wheel.

"Want me to drive?" Bobby asked.

I turned onto a deserted dirt road, stopped the car,

turned off the radio, and burst into tears. Bobby rubbed my shoulder.

"I'm sorry," I blubbered. "I'm sorry."

"Shh, shh," he whispered. I cried, and he rubbed my shoulder.

"I don't talk about her to anyone but Gail," I gasped. "My father acts as if everything is normal. He sometimes talks about After. That means After she dies. But he never says, 'She's dying.' And she is." I sobbed some more. "And the worst part is, I can't even talk to her."

"What do you mean?"

I told him what she'd been like when I visited her.

"Oh, my God, how awful," he said. "You can't even say good-bye."

"Or say I'm sorry," I cried.

"Sorry?"

"For being nasty, snotty, contemptuous of her," I whispered.

Silence.

"You mean, a teenager," he said.

Yes. Exactly.

"I don't think it's easy no matter how it happens," he said. "Even if you had months to say good-bye, you would still feel like you hadn't done enough."

Silence.

"My best friend's father was sick with cancer for

months before he died. So I speak from experience," he said. "In the end, it's just awful, no matter what."

Silence.

"I feel like someone covered my eyeballs with cheesecloth. And my eardrums, too, sometimes. Like I am surrounded by fog, like I live in a cumulonimbus cloud."

Silence. Good silence.

"How is your friend now?" I asked.

"You mean, how long does it take to get over it?"

"Yeah, I guess."

"I think it's always there," he said softly. "Only the sharpness of it gets dulled."

"Oh."

We sat together for a while.

"It's cold," I said.

"And getting dark," Bobby said.

I turned the car back on, and the radio. We drove home in silence. Comfortable.

I dropped Bobby off at his house and just made it home before it got completely dark. A friend, I thought. A friend who is a boy.

My father was waiting for me in the living room.

"I just got the phone call, Neenie."

"The phone call?"

"From the doctor," he said. "She's gone."

My mother. He's saying my mother is dead.

"You mean Mommy?" I asked.

"Yes," he said.

Say it. Say, "Your mom is dead."

"She's gone," he said.

Before it was After. Now it's Gone.

"Oh," I said.

"I called Ben and Harry. They'll call everyone else. People will start to come over soon."

"Oh," I said.

He walked toward me and put his hands lightly on my shoulders. He stood there. I put my arms around him. I wanted to hug him tight, to hold on. My daddy, my daddy, my daddy. But he's hollow, I thought. My arms rested stiffly on his waist. We stayed that way, each of us staring into space, past each other.

"Okay," he said, and walked out.

I had been waiting for him to cry. But of course he never cried. He had no tears. "Pissy eyes," he called anyone who did.

I went upstairs to my room. I took my brush and brushed and brushed my hair. I bent forward and brushed from back to front, then front to back. I did it again. I sat down at my vanity table and looked at myself in the mirror. Madame Lebrun's daughter, without Madame Lebrun.

I took off my red sweater and looked through my closet. I couldn't wear red now. But I had nothing black to wear. I owned nothing black. What was I going to wear to the funeral? Why hadn't I thought of that before? Gray is all right. I'll wear gray. Gray like the ocean at Cape Cod. I found a gray cardigan. I put on a white blouse with the gray cardigan over it. I put on my gray knee socks and pulled them up, sitting down on my bed to straighten them. I turned the cuffs over twice, neatly. The ribs had to be straight; the cuffs had to be narrow and rolled over two times; the elastic had to be good enough to keep the socks up. I would need new knee socks soon. I'd have to buy them myself now. I took some rubber bands off the doorknob and put them under the cuffs just to make sure. Good. I put my gray pleated skirt on and looked in the mirror to see how many times I had to roll up the waist. Two times took the skirt to just in the middle of my knees. Three times took it above them. Too high. Two times. Now I was all in gray. Good. I sat on my bed, picked up my mother's tweezers, pulled my right knee sock down and started plucking the hairs from the inside of my calf. I lined up the hairs on the edge of my white pillowcase. Some were long and thin, some short and fat. The fatter ones hurt more. I had a long line of hairs, an army of them lined up, when I heard Gert's voice. I brushed all the hairs away, pulled up my knee sock, and went downstairs.

# CHAPTER NINE

LATE THAT NIGHT I sat on my bed again, looking out at my tree. The moon was shining, turning its icy bare limbs silvery. I couldn't sleep, and I couldn't think. I roamed around my room, looking at my books, my records, my clothes. I tiptoed downstairs to the kitchen. All the dishes were clean, left drying on the counter. My mother never left dishes out like that. But they weren't her dishes now.

I went into the living room and sat down on the couch. The moonlight streamed in through the picture window. My mother hadn't closed the curtains. I sat there, looking around the room. The women who had come with food had washed all the ashtrays and put them back, but they were not in their right places. I got up and moved them to where they belonged. I sat down again and opened the candy dish. It was full of pistachio nuts, full to the brim. Who had put them there? That was the M&M's dish. The pistachios went in the wooden bowl with the top that stuck, the one that belonged on the end table next to my father's chair. This

123

was all wrong. My mother's living room had been violated. I sat and glared at the M&M's dish, stupidly, thoughtlessly, insanely filled with pistachio nuts.

Earlier that evening, before everyone arrived, Gert had been in the kitchen with Ruth and Esther, my mother's best friends, getting glasses and dishes out and taking them to the dining room. Gert had hugged me when I walked in. Then Ruth, then Esther. I helped them with the good silverware.

Gert put her arm around my shoulder and steered me into a corner of the kitchen. "I probably shouldn't say this to you, Mindy, but I think I owe it to my friend, to your mother."

I stared at her.

"Your father just told me your grandmother, your mother's mother, isn't coming to the funeral."

Not *the* funeral, my mother's funeral.

"Not coming to your mother's funeral," she said.

"Yes?"

"This doesn't surprise you, does it?" she asked. Tears welled up in her eyes. Live tears, not like the tears in the white room.

"No," I said. I hadn't really thought about it. Grandma hadn't come when Mom got sick, when she was operated on. Why should she come now?

"Her own daughter," Gert was saying. "Her only

daughter, her only child, after she buried her only son."

I remembered once when we were visiting my grandmother in Florida, my mother pulled the blinds in my room and knocked them, just softly, against the wall. Grandma had looked to see if the paint on the wall had chipped and said something, I don't remember what. It could have been "Oh." And my mother had screamed at her, screamed that she had already buried a son, did she want to bury her daughter, too? That was the only time I ever heard Mom raise her voice to her mother.

"I have to say this to you, Mindy, for you and for your mother's memory. Your grandmother is loveless. She is frozen. I always felt that, but now I am certain. Her own daughter sick. Her own daughter dying. Her own daughter dead. And she stays in Florida." The tears spilled down Gert's cheeks. "All those letters your mother wrote her. All those unanswered letters." She hugged me. "I am so sorry, Mindy. So sorry."

I nestled my head in between her enormous breasts and felt safe.

"Thank you," I whispered. "Thank you for saying it out loud."

More people started arriving. Everyone brought a big pot or plate of food. Had they all been cooking quantities of food that afternoon? Had they cooked this food weeks ago, when the biopsy came back, frozen it, and just reheated it? I kept saying "thank you, thank you," and everyone kept saying "I'm so sorry, so sorry," and handing me bowls and platters and casseroles of food. Who was supposed to eat all of it?

My father was sitting in his chair in the living room, smoking and talking. "Why do they call it a living room?" I remembered Andrew asking. "Hasn't anyone ever died in one?"

My father looked as he always did. How could she be dead if he still looked the same? How could he look the same if she was dead? I stayed with the women, carrying dishes back and forth between the kitchen and the dining room. Thank God there was something to do. More and more people arrived, bringing more and more food, saying how sorry they were.

A tiny old woman came in the back door. I was alone in the kitchen. I recognized her but didn't know from where. She put a big casserole on the kitchen table and took my face in her hands.

"She was a wonderful woman," she whispered. "A wonderful woman. So kind and considerate. I'm sorry. I'm so sorry."

"Thank you," I said. "Thank you."

"She was always so nice to me. Always." She hugged me and left.

I went out into the dining room, and then it hit me. She was Mrs. Brown, the candy store man's wife. I saw her in the back room of the store every so often. I never knew she knew my mother at all.

People kept coming up to me, hugging me and saying how sorry they were. And I kept saying "thank you" over and over. I kept wanting to say how sorry *I* was, but it didn't seem right. "Thank you" seemed to be the right thing to say. I could hear my mother's voice saying it, "Thank you, thank you." My father was still sitting in his chair, still smoking, still looking the same. Everyone was eating, talking softly, glancing at me, hugging me, eating. It was as if someone had turned the volume down. Everything looked normal, but the sound was muted. Death did this, set all this weirdness in motion, made people appear out of nowhere carrying casseroles, saying "I'm sorry" over and over, death muffled their voices. Impersonal, generalized death, the death from John Donne's sonnet starting "Death be not proud." Not my mother's death, just death itself taking over.

I saw Gail making her way through the crowd, looking for me. I pushed past whoever I was saying "thank you" to and ran into Gail's arms. She hugged me hard, and I hugged her back.

"Can we go for a walk around the block?" she whispered.

"Thank you," I said. I got my coat, and we went out the side door. "Phew." We breathed in the cold, cold air. "What a relief. I couldn't take much more. I didn't know what to say to anyone, and there was so much food I was getting nauseous looking at it."

We walked down my block without saying anything, the crisp top layer of snow crunching under our feet. The air smelled so clean, so new, so fresh.

"When do you suppose this will feel real?" I asked.

Silence.

"You wouldn't believe the songs running through my head," I said.

"Bet I would," Gail said. "The one about the motherless child?"

"You are amazing." I laughed. "And here's a really sick one: 'Goodbye Cruel World.' "

"The one where he goes off to join the army or the circus?"

"It doesn't matter."

Silence.

"Once, a few years ago, she was interviewing a woman for a job as our cleaning lady. I pretended I was asleep on the couch. I couldn't imagine what she would say to the woman. And I don't remember what she did say. But at the end the woman stood up and said, 'I don't think this would work out for me. You are *sooo* high-strung,' and she left. I was embarrassed for my mother and confused about what *high-strung* meant. I couldn't believe that someone who walked into our house for ten minutes could form an impression of my mother so quickly. It was weird. But she was right. She was high-strung. I could see it later."

"Yes, she was," Gail said. "And she loved you very much."

I stopped walking and stared at her.

"How do you know that?" I whispered.

"It was so obvious. Just as obvious as the fact that she was high-strung." Gail put her arm around my shoulder, and I burst into tears. She held me and let me cry all over her coat. Then she gave me a Kleenex, and I blew my nose. I blew it really loud, in the soft, quiet night. We started walking again.

"Do you remember your father?" I asked.

"Yeah. After he died, I was afraid I would forget him, even forget what he looked like, so I made my mother put that picture of him in my room. Now that's how I remember him looking, that picture. But I felt like without it, he'd start to fade."

Silence.

"But I never forgot his smell. That never faded. And the sound of his laugh."

Silence.

"Since I saw Mom the last time in the hospital, that's the only way I remember her. In that white room. Not my mother at all."

Silence.

"But I do remember her smell."

"Jean Naté." We both laughed.

"But under the Jean Naté, you know? Her real smell. I can still smell that."

*Crunch-crunch* went the snow beneath our shoes.

"Do you remember my bride doll?" I asked.

"Yes, she was gorgeous. She had real hair."

"And do you remember how I never played with her? She came with a tiny suitcase and tiny hair curlers. You were supposed to wash and set her hair. I never did. I was afraid I'd ruin her. I never even took off her bride's dress. I left the suitcase tied to her wrist, with the tiny hair curlers inside. They were pink."

Silence.

"I feel the same way about my mother. Like I never really gave her a chance, never really played with her, you know? I just tested her."

"Remember how she gave you a surprise twelfth birthday party because you said you wanted a surprise party?" Gail asked.

"Yes."

"She called me every day, checking to make sure she had invited everybody, that the sleigh ride idea was a good one, to ask me what you wanted as a present."

"I didn't know that," I said. There was so much I didn't know.

"She did. She drove me nuts, asking me everything, wanting it to be just what you wanted."

"Then why didn't you tell her that pizza and cocoa is a terrible combination?"

We laughed, and then we both cried.

"The night before I went to sleep-away camp for the first time, she told me that when she had gone to camp, her mother told her that she'd be homesick and that that was all right, to be expected. But when she went to camp, she wasn't homesick, she loved being at camp, and then she felt terrible that she didn't miss her mother. So she wanted me to know that it was okay not to be homesick, that it was okay to have a great time at camp and not to think about home at all. . . . She tried so hard not to be like her mother," I added.

"You're a lot alike," said Gail.

"Trying not to be like our mothers, you mean?"

"Yep."

Silence.

I heard someone's footsteps, and we both turned

131

around. Bobby was walking toward us, his hands in his pockets, head thrust forward. We waited for him. He put his arms around me and hugged me tight.

"How did you find us?" I asked when he let me go.

"I went to your house, and someone told me you two had gone for a walk. I thought I wouldn't be able to find you, but I did."

"We've been walking around and around the block," Gail said. "Like we were too young to cross the street." We all laughed and started to walk again, me safe in the middle, all three of us holding hands.

"Where do you think she is now?" I asked, looking up at the sky. "Is she on her way up to heaven?"

"Yes," said Gail. "And she is whole now. She can see and hear and think. God has taken her and made her whole."

"I wish I were Catholic and believed all that," I said, and cried again. The two of them hugged me. "I didn't think it would feel different when she actually died. I felt like I had gotten used to it, used to not having her here. But it's different now. It's so different." I cried and cried.

"I don't think you ever believe in death until it happens. Even if you know and know that the person is *going* to die," Bobby said. "I think you always believe it won't really happen—until it really does."

"I guess that's what 'Hope springs eternal' means," said Gail.

"I always thought that was about an artesian well," I said.

Bobby said, "I always thought it was about a cat named Hope who always pounced."

"That's what makes horse races," Gail and I said together, and we laughed.

We started to walk again, crunching along, holding mittened hands, me still snug in the middle. I squeezed their hands, one, two, three times. I love you. And they squeezed back.

∾

This stupid candy dish. I was still holding the top by its pointy little black handle. Filled with pistachio nuts. It was so wrong. It was all so wrong. I raised the top over my head. I'll smash it. I'll smash the whole stupid dish. I hate it. I'll smash it and throw away all the pieces. I'll never have to see it again. And then I saw the crack in one of the little black claw feet. A diagonal line across one foot. My mother had glued that claw back together when I was little. She had gotten special ceramic glue. I looked at the lid. And she had glued the lid back together, too. You could see the crack across the whole white inside of the lid. I turned the lid over. She had matched the swirly green and yellow outside pattern perfectly. You could only see the crack on the inside. I put the lid gently down on top of the bowl. I'll fill it up with M&M's, Mama. I'll fix it tomorrow.

I'm sorry. I'm sorry I was so mad at you. I'm sorry I'm still so mad at you.

I always thought my life was normal, common. Nothing exciting ever happened. Nothing out of the ordinary. But now I have no mother. That is out of the ordinary. That is not the way it should be. That is not fair. Even if I was mean to you so much, didn't want you interfering in my life, hated the way you dressed, made fun of your sense of humor. Even though I did all that, it's still not fair that I lost you. I know you didn't die on purpose. I know it's not your fault. But I do so want to blame someone. The only ones are me or you, and I don't want to pick either of us. So it just has to be that life is not fair. Really not fair. Not fair for either of us. You don't get to see me as an adult, and I don't get to have you with me at graduation, on the day I get into college, on the day I go to college. I'm on my own now. That's what I thought I wanted for so long. And now that I am, I miss you more than I ever thought I could.

I have missed you for so long. At first it was because I threw you away. My phase, you called it. Being a teenager, Bobby calls it. And then you got sick. One for me, one for you. I can't seem to get away from blaming. Who do *you* blame, Mama? Do you blame me? Dad? Yourself? Your mother? God? Do you ask, "Who did this to me?" Do you ask, "Why?"

Gail says these things take time. I hope she's right. She says you are whole now, your eyes can see, you can think, you can feel, you are not the woman in the white room anymore. I hope she's right about that, too.

I can't take care of Dad for you, Mama. You did such a good job, and I can't. He doesn't love me. I know, I know, he loves me in his own way. But his own way has so little to do with me it doesn't feel like love at all. I know you love him, and I don't know why. Except that he loves you. I guess that's a good reason. But I'm not you, Mama. And he is not like that with me. I'm sorry. I know you would like us to be close again, like when I was little. But he only wants to be close to Neenie, the three-year-old me, not the one who lives in my skin now. I don't think he even sees me, the now me. Every time he looks at me, he sees Neenie, the child who adored him, who ran to the door when he came home, yelling, "My daddy, my daddy, my daddy!" not the sixteen-year-old he dropped when she was twelve, not Mindy. I have to take care of Mindy now, I have to take care of me. And I have Gail and Bobby. And Andrew. They help. They will help.

Here's a promise for you, Mama. And for me, too. When I grow up and have a daughter, I will tell her all about you, like you told me all about Irving. And I'll sit with her at my mirror, holding her, and we will both say, "Madame Lebrun and her daughter." And I will teach her how to say I love you by squeezing hands.